His Little Runaway

Emily Tilton

Copyright © 2016 by Emily Tilton

Published by Stormy Night Publications and Design, LLC.
www.StormyNightPublications.com

Cover design by Korey Mae Johnson
www.koreymaejohnson.com

Images by Bigstock/Wisky, 123RF/Nophamon Yanyapong, and 123RF/sondem

All rights reserved.

1st Print Edition. May 2016

ISBN-13: 978-1533183392

ISBN-10: 1533183392

FOR AUDIENCES 18+ ONLY

This book is intended for adults only. Spanking and other sexual activities represented in this book are fantasies only, intended for adults.

CHAPTER ONE

Ashley stumbled through the trees, desperately wondering if she could make it to the road she knew must lie ahead of her, up the slope. She had even thought she saw headlights a few minutes before, though the flash of illumination through the thick, bare branches had come and gone so quickly that she mistrusted her mind's interpretation of her senses' information.

She mistrusted everything about her mind and her body; both were much, much too tired to give reliable data. Her feet—in sneakers never intended even to take five steps in six-inch-deep snow, let alone run more than a mile through it—were soaking and numb. At least the temperature had gone above freezing the previous day, or Ashley thought she probably wouldn't have lasted a quarter mile.

But of course the slight melting of the snow made everything slushy and wet, and now it seemed a question not of whether she could make it to the road but of whether the dogs would find her before she fell down and made their job all too easy. And of course when the dogs did arrive she would feel grateful to be alive.

The warden would say that, too, wouldn't he? "Young lady, you should feel grateful to be alive."

They would bring her back. They would put her in solitary again. After three days, she would be grateful not just to be alive but to have the warden bring her to his office for a special session. The way it had happened to Jenny, right after she turned eighteen.

"It's not so bad, sucking his cock," Jenny had said. But Jenny's eyes had told Ashley everything she needed to know when Ms. Barnes, who taught the computer class they were making her take, told Ashley that the warden wanted to see her.

And the warden himself hadn't even tried to conceal his intentions much. Since the private company had taken over at Tall Oaks Juvenile Correction Facility, Ashley had been shocked on an almost daily basis by how little care the teachers and correctional officers seemed to show about covering up their abuses: the brutal way the new guards broke up fights, the cutting back of class hours. The special sessions in the warden's office.

"Ashley, I want to make something very clear to you," the warden said once she had sat in the metal chair across his desk from him. "I can make your life very difficult, now that you're one of the girls we keep from ages eighteen to twenty-one."

Most of the time, since the terrible night she had crashed her cute red convertible into the police car a month before her eighteenth birthday, she had responded with an attitude she called, to herself, *Westchester pride*. Ashley came from Westchester County. Her parents had given her everything she wanted and needed, including the cute red convertible. She knew full well that the world regarded her as a spoiled brat, no one more than her teachers here at Tall Oaks Juvie.

From the moment it had become clear to Ashley Lewis that a juvenile correctional facility lay in her future, she had adopted Westchester pride as her defense. She had perfect manners; her mother had seen to that. She would never disobey, but she would also never show anyone from this horrible broken system anything more than the bare

modicum of respect needed to keep out of solitary.

Ashley didn't need computer classes, and she needed the English and Social Studies classes even less. She would go to college when she got out, in a year. Her parents had told her that. Even if what the academic classes at Tall Oaks covered had offered anything Ashley hadn't covered in her sophomore year of high school, she would have refused to do anything but try as hard as she could to get D's instead of the A's she could have achieved with ridiculous ease.

"I know, sir," Ashley replied to the warden, respecting him with her words but disrespecting him with her eyes, despite how frightened she was. Really she should be able to turn off the Westchester pride, shouldn't she? But it had become nearly automatic.

"Do you want me to make your life difficult, Ashley? I believe Ms. Barnes said you talked back to her in class on Monday. I could isolate you for that."

"No, sir." Ashley swallowed.

"No, you don't want me to make your life difficult? Or, no, you didn't sass Ms. Barnes?" The warden, slightly paunchy and very greasy, got up from behind his desk and hitched up his belt. His badge clinked against a gold ring on his left hand: a wedding ring.

"Neither, sir." Now, as she quailed back against the hard metal of the chair, Ashley tried everything she could to make herself respectful. It was probably the wrong decision, but there probably didn't exist a single right one. At any rate, the warden seemed to grow in satisfaction and in authority as he noticed the effect he had on her. He sauntered around to the front of his desk and leaned against it. His crotch, covered in the blue wool of his trousers, loomed a foot away from Ashley's face.

"Alright, then. I want you to think about what you're willing to do for me, so that I don't make your life difficult."

"Like what, sir?" Her voice trembled.

"I'm sure an eighteen-year-old suburban slut like you can think of what she should be ready to do for a man who

knows how to treat her. What happens in my office stays in my office. When you come back here Friday for your first special session, I want you to be ready to show me something I'd like to see, and to take what I have to give you. You'll take off your shirt so I can play with those sweet young tits of yours, and you'll learn to give a proper blowjob. We'll have a good time, and you'll have extra privileges. I'll tell Ms. Barnes to go easy on you."

He laid all this out there so very blandly. Ashley felt her breath coming in sharp little gasps, but the warden seemed not even to notice that he had proposed to abuse one of the girls he was supposed to be taking care of. The shock of it—despite knowing, from Jenny, that this was probably coming—felt so deep that Ashley began to feel like she didn't even inhabit her own body.

"Or," the warden continued, "you know, isolating you isn't even the worst thing I can do, Ashley. If I have to, I can discipline you the old-fashioned way, on your impudent bare backside. The old paddle is still here in my office. When you come back, I can bend you over this desk and take down your panties for punishment, if that's what it takes. Some girls need that, and I don't mind giving a hiding—especially when a girl's backside is as pretty as yours."

It didn't even seem worth mentioning the illegality of it, and the bruises she could show to anyone at Tall Oaks—no one at Tall Oaks would care.

If she made it to the road, managed to flag someone down, she might well thank the warden in her heart that he was such a bastard that he enjoyed making girls like Ashley think his abusive propositions over before their first special sessions with him. As she stumbled through the woods, she wished only that she had tried this insane escape the first night, rather than lying awake in bed all night. She might not be so tired, then.

There: headlights again. The road must be only fifty feet up the slope, which had gotten much steeper, though the trees had thinned out to scrub bushes that Ashley clawed

desperately at for purchase.

The guardrail. More headlights. Which way was Tall Oaks? Which way was the nearest gas station? How could Ashley have any idea? She could beg for a cell phone, call her parents. They could start an investigation about Tall Oaks. She wouldn't have to go back there.

Car. Cell phone.

Over the guardrail. She didn't mean to fall down into the road, but she did. On her side, looking into the oncoming headlights.

The headlights, much too close. A scream of rubber stopping sharply on asphalt. The burning smell of the rubber, coming to her nostrils.

A moment in which she had probably been unconscious.

"Are you okay? What the hell do you think you're doing?" A deep, worried voice.

Knees, squatting, in jeans that looked faded in the glare of the headlights. Raising her head feebly, but only catching a hint of flannel shirt.

"Can you talk? What's your name, honey? Don't move. We have to make sure nothing's broken."

The story she had made up as she lay awake, waiting to get up and make her run for it, began to come out. "Help me, please," she said through practically numb lips.

"I'll do my best, honey," said the deep voice. "It looks like you can move your head, but you've got some really bad scrapes on your face. Try sitting up."

Was that the baying of a dog over the sound of the pickup?

"Have to go," she mumbled. She did try to sit up, and succeeded after one false start. She felt sore all over, especially the side of her face where it had impacted the road as she had come over the guardrail.

Ashley looked into the eyes of a tall, heavily muscled man. Her first, dismayed thought was that he must be an off-duty guard from Tall Oaks, but she didn't recognize him, and he didn't recognize her. He had close-cropped

dark hair and a chiseled jaw with a day or two's growth of beard.

"Take it easy," he said. "I'm Wes. What's your name?"

"Please," Ashley said, "can we go? Can you take me to a gas station, maybe?"

A puzzled expression came over Wes' face in the glow of his pickup truck's headlights. Ashley noticed that above him, the sky seemed less dark than it had been a few minutes before as she had clambered up the slope.

"Why?" Wes said. The confusion turned to suspicion. "What are you running from? Shouldn't I take you to the police, if you're running from someone?"

Ashley bit her lip and gave the answer she had ready. "He's a cop. Please, just take me... somewhere. I need to talk to my parents."

Wes nodded. "Alright. I'll take you to my house. It's not much farther away than the nearest gas station. Can you get up?"

He put his arm around Ashley and got her to her feet. She had banged her hip, falling into the road, she realized now, and so she was grateful for his helping her into the high cab of the truck. She thought she heard another bark of a dog, though, and so it seemed like forever went by while he closed the passenger door and walked around to the driver's side. After he climbed in, Wes reached behind his seat and came up with a roll of paper towels. He handed it to her.

"Hold some of these against your face and try to press down a little, okay?"

"Okay," she replied. "I'm Ashley," she said after he had put the truck in gear and started up down the dark road.

"What's a pretty girl like you doing falling into a road in a place like this?"

Wes' truck had already gone half a mile through the pre-dawn of the upstate New York woods. Had she really done it? The fear and elation that filled her chest in equal measure made it difficult to concentrate on what Wes had just said.

"I…" She realized her teeth had started to chatter.

"Shh," Wes said, glancing over. He turned the heat up. "That's okay. You just curl up there and go to sleep if you can. We've got an hour or so to drive. We can talk later."

"Okay," Ashley said. She must be in shock, or something. Everything seemed so far away. She curled up as the cab of the pickup got warmer. The big man—the big, kind man—next to her in the red flannel shirt looked at the road. Wes.

Then the truck was pulling up in front of a cabin, with snowy trees looming all around. Wes turned the key and looked at her, saw she had woken up. "My place," he said. "Let's get you inside and clean you up."

CHAPTER TWO

Wes Garner knew Ashley had probably lied to him. That didn't mean he shouldn't patch her up before he decided what to do about it, though. At least she didn't seem to have broken anything in that crazy fall into the road. He shook his head, remembering, as he got the washcloths out of the linen closet. You never knew when trained reflexes would save someone's life, he supposed, but he hadn't expected to be saving a girl half jumping, half crashing into the pavement in front of his pickup at four o'clock in the morning on a deserted forest road.

He filled a basin with warm water and got the soap and bandages from the bathroom. He found Ashley sitting where he had left her on the living room couch, making a rather adorable effort not to bleed on his furniture and looking around at the furnishings of the neat little cabin. It wasn't much, but Wes felt a good deal of pride in how well he kept it.

"Made the furniture myself," he said, knowing that Ashley's eyes were probably fixed not on the oak chairs but on the pictures of Wes and his buddies at camp.

"You're in the army?" she asked.

Wes laughed despite the pang he always felt when

someone pursued this line of questioning. "Was. Not army. The navy."

He squatted in front of her.

"Turn your face to the right, honey," he said. She obeyed, and he looked critically at the laceration over her cheekbone. "This is gonna hurt when I clean it out," he said, "but it looks a lot worse than it is."

"Okay," Ashley said. "If you were in the navy, why aren't you, you know, on a boat in the pictures?"

He laughed again, but didn't answer until he started to clean the scrape with his washcloth. Ashley bit her lip at the pain, and her eyes watered, but she didn't make a sound.

"Well, I started out on a boat, but then I trained as a SEAL."

"A Navy SEAL?" Ashley said. "Really?" The awe in her voice gratified Wes as much as it distressed him. No matter how it had all ended, and no matter that he lived like a woodworking hermit in the Adirondacks: it had happened, and what he had done, he had done to uphold the values he still held dear.

"Yup," Wes said. "So tell me what happened. Why were you running through the woods?" He dabbed Vaseline on her face. "This is going to look really bad in the mirror for a day or two, but I promise it'll heal better with the Vaseline instead of a bandage."

"Um," Ashley said. "Okay."

"Show me your hands. You were gonna tell me why you jumped into the road right in front of me and nearly got yourself run over."

Wes didn't feel completely sure that Ashley *had* intended to tell him that—despite his asking. But as she extended her hands, where he could see that she had taken the skin off the finger and palms in several painful-looking places, she said in much too pat a way, "My boyfriend. He hurts me. He's a cop, so I can't go to the cops."

"Local or state?" Wes asked. He looked up from where he was using a fresh washcloth to clean the dirt out of a

laceration on her left palm. Long, currently very dirty, chestnut hair framed a very pretty heart-shaped face, currently marred a bit by the scrape on her left cheekbone. Green eyes, currently featuring deep purple circles of exhaustion beneath them. A startled, very worried expression.

She didn't even think to decide whether this fake boyfriend is a local cop or a state trooper.

"Local," she finally said, blinking.

"We'll call the district attorney," Wes said, to see what Ashley would say in response.

It appeared she had thought of this part. She lied—if she was lying, which Wes felt upwards of 90% certain was the case—smoothly now. "He's got, you know, friends in all those offices. I need to call my parents. They live in Westchester."

"Oh," Wes said, feeling his mouth crook into a little smile. "Westchester."

Ashley nodded. The vulnerability in her face had flown away, and now despite the cut her face assumed a kind of bored, set expression that seemed to say that no guy who lived in the woods and made furniture, even if he'd once been a Navy SEAL, should get it in his head to ask questions of a girl who came from Westchester.

Wes wasn't surprised to find that the emerging brat in Ashley brought out his instinctive desire to set her straight. He decided to keep that desire in check at least for the moment. Maybe she just needed sleep, and would be kinder when she'd had a few hours of it. He had to say that the hard expression on her face seemed a little too well-practiced for that, though.

"You can call your folks when you've had some sleep," he said, wrapping a bandage around her hand.

"Why not now?" Ashley asked sharply. *Definitely bratty.*

"No phone. I'll have to walk you up to the top of the driveway to get cell reception, and then you can use my cell."

She looked at him suspiciously. "I want to call now. I... want them to know I'm alright."

Her lies seemed to be coming less smoothly. Wasn't there a juvenile facility around that place where he had picked her up?

"You can barely keep your eyes open, honey," Wes said in a reassuring voice. "You won't be able to make it up the driveway."

"Can't you drive me?"

"You need sleep, Ashley. A couple of hours won't make a difference." Now he spoke in a more authoritative way, even letting some of his daddy side come out in his tone and the way he looked at her.

Ashley's brow furrowed, but the hard expression also seemed to leave her face. "Okay," she said. "But... please wake me up in an hour? And take me up there, so I can call?"

"Two hours," Wes said firmly. "One hour won't do you any good at all. Trust me. I know sleep deprivation."

Ashley's eyes widened. "Why did you leave the navy?"

"Long story," Wes said, starting to help her to her feet to walk her into the bedroom. When he got her there, he turned down the comforter and the sheet, fighting a sudden urge to offer to help Ashley undress. Instead he got a t-shirt from his dresser and handed it to her.

"Lay your clothes out on the bed once you've gotten out of them and into this. I'll wash them while you're sleeping."

"Okay," Ashley said, looking down at the t-shirt. Was she thinking, as Wes couldn't help thinking, about how cute and little-girlish she would look in it, with only her panties underneath? She looked up at him. "Thank you for picking me up on the road."

"You're welcome. Now you get into bed as soon as I go, alright?" He couldn't help it: the daddy definitely came out in the way he said that. To his surprise, Ashley's face broke into a little instinctive smile as if at the sound of the paternal admonition.

"Alright," she said with a yawn.

Wes went to his truck to get the hardware he'd been hauling back from Ohio: antique nails he could have had them ship to him, but Wes liked to handle everything he put into his furniture, and he felt like it made a difference in the quality. By the time he'd put the box in his workshop, a roomy shed detached from the cabin, and gone to check on Ashley, she had fallen asleep. He picked up her jeans, long-sleeved t-shirt, and underwear, noticing to his surprise that she had taken off everything, including a pair of light blue nylon panties that he tried to hide under the shirt so he wouldn't think about her being naked under his t-shirt.

He put the clothes in the washing machine, turned it on. He got his cell phone and started out into the chilly dawn.

Once he got to the top of the driveway it didn't take him long to figure out who she was: the news was plastered across the website of the local newspaper.

The escapee, identified as Ashley Lewis, 18, originally of Pelham, is not considered dangerous, but citizens are advised not to attempt to apprehend her but to report any sighting to the police at the following number.

Reached for a statement in Albany, the head of the department of corrections said she would call for an inquiry into the circumstances of Lewis' escape. "It's too early to know anything, but of course we need to determine the causes and assign responsibility for this unfortunate occurrence."

Wes shook his head as he turned off the phone. From the top of the driveway, he could look east across the whole of the little valley where he had built himself a new life after the navy, into the perfect pink ball of the rising sun.

This unfortunate occurrence. Had they used words like that when they'd decided his fate? No, *violation of the rules of engagement* had been more the speed of the court-martial.

He had saved Marmara, though. In Wes' blackest moments, he wondered whether he had done the wrong

thing. He didn't care about the rules of engagement—he hadn't cared about them since the moment Marmara told him, weeping hysterically, that her uncle had sold her virginity to the warlord, and the warlord had decided she would marry his cousin.

Marmara: just eighteen, like Ashley Lewis. A sweet tooth like nothing Wes had ever seen, and a smile that said *princess* and *brat* but also *sweetheart* and *baby doll*. Teaching her to pronounce *Wesley* in her musical accent.

"May I call you *daddy*? I've always wanted a daddy, Wesley."

He felt a little pang in his heart for this orphan whose eyes always seemed bright nevertheless. "Call me *sugar daddy*, honey," he had replied, grinning. "I don't think I can ever give you as much candy as I'd like to."

"You can try," Marmara said, pouting.

"Do you need a spanking, young lady?" Wes asked playfully. "Where I come from, girls who pout get something to cry about."

He hadn't known where that had come from, really, about the spanking. He had heard of ageplay, and he had known he might want to try it someday, but Marmara seemed to bring out a side of him he had thought might lurk in his fantasies but which had never shown itself to anyone—even Wes himself—before.

And on one level, as he said it, it had felt so wrong. Marmara had lost her parents to a bomb before she was four years old. Corporal punishment of the worst kind—the kind given just to prove that the person with the cane had power and the person, especially the woman, crying as the cane fell over and over, did not—made a fundamental note in family life in Marmara's world.

Nevertheless, he saw something light up in Marmara's eyes. "What's a spanking?" she asked, though Wes knew that she, a very bright girl, must know.

"Come here," he said, "and I'll show you." Wes was standing in the road, and Marmara in the little garden she

tended every day.

He didn't expect her to come, but she did, first looking around to make sure no one from her family could see. She crossed the five feet or so to stand in front of him, a mischievous look on her face.

"Show me, daddy," she said, looking up at him with a little smile.

He knew he couldn't, as much as he wanted to. He would have loved to bare her bottom and turn her over his knee, the way discipline from a daddy should always be given, but he had seen enough of Marmara's culture to know that the consequences of that for her could be terrible. Really, he needed to put a stop to this; he couldn't even turn her around and give her the swat over her clothes that he wanted to give her.

"I think you know, honey," he said, smiling warmly.

"What if I do?" A very bratty expression now.

"If you're telling a fib, no more candy."

"Fib?" Now Wes could tell she really didn't know that word. He chuckled and pulled a chocolate bar out of his pocket.

"A little lie, honey. What you just did when you pretended you didn't know what a spanking was."

Walking down to the cabin, remembering Marmara and wondering what to do about Ashley, he stopped his mind from going back to what had happened only a week later: Marmara in tears. Not *an unfortunate occurrence* but an act of anger and of justice. A *violation*. But he had saved Marmara, and he would do it again.

Wes doubted whether saving Ashley Lewis would be anything near as straightforward.

CHAPTER THREE

Ashley woke up to find that someone was rubbing her shoulder. No bell. No faint smell of sewage covered by the stronger, harsher smell of disinfectant. A warm comforter, not a scratchy blanket.

She opened her eyes to look into the face of a man whose name it took her a moment to remember. *Wes*. She felt like she had been asleep for days. Her whole body hurt, but she also felt like a fuzziness that had descended more and more upon her, ever since the warden had made it clear she would service him or pay the consequences of refusal, had lifted, and she could think straight.

What had she told him? The abusive boyfriend story she had concocted, she felt almost certain. And he had said that she could use his cell phone at the top of his driveway. She felt her eyes go wide as the memories came flooding back. She knew she couldn't let down her guard, but despite what seemed a rather stern expression in Wes' eyes Ashley felt a rush of gratitude toward him.

"Thanks," she said. "I mean, thanks for picking me up, and…" She remembered about her hands and lifted them up to see the bandages wrapped around them. They hurt terribly, but he must have put some kind of salve on that

made them feel more like a dull ache than a burning fire.

"You're welcome," Wes said gravely. "I've put your clothes on top of the dresser."

Ashley remembered suddenly that, unsure of whether to do so or not, she had taken off her panties and put them in with the jeans and shirt and bra. Now she suddenly wished she had kept the underwear on—she could have washed them herself by hand or something, rather than feel first like Wes had handled her panties and second like she now didn't have any on underneath the big red t-shirt he had loaned her.

Now she started to wonder what her face looked like, and her hair. She must look beyond awful, and she realized that with the Vaseline on her face she must have ruined his pillowcase. She propped herself up on her elbow to look, and saw that Wes had put a soft towel down under her cheek, where she could see a little bit of gory mess.

"Oh," she said.

Wes must have followed her look, since he said, "I hope the towel wasn't uncomfortable."

Ashley searched her mind for any memory of the sleep she'd just had, but found an utter blank. "Nope," she said.

"Alright, then. I've got breakfast almost ready. When you get dressed, come on into the kitchen."

For the first time Ashley realized then that instead of the smells of Tall Oaks she could make out the heavenly scent of real bacon.

"Can I call my parents first?"

"Nope," Wes replied. "I need to be sure you're steady on your feet, and for that I need to get some food into you.

What was it about the way he spoke to her, with such decision, that seemed to make her trust him? When one was a juvenile offender, men often addressed you as if they were in charge of you—because of course they were. Most recently, the warden had done that. Ashley should be used to—if not resisting the will of big men who ordered her around—at least maintaining her Westchester pride. Why

did she feel like contradicting Wes would be different? Like she *wanted* to contradict him, but not so that she wouldn't have to obey him; rather, so that he would make it clear to her that he would give her breakfast, *now*, whether she liked it or not?

"Okay," she said, and started to climb out of bed.

"Bathroom's next door," he informed her, once she was on her feet and he could look her up and down. To her annoyance, Ashley blushed, thinking again about her panties—about Wes touching them and her currently not having them on, under the t-shirt. "Don't take a shower, though. You can do that after breakfast. I need to take a look at your wounds and clean them before you get in the shower."

"Okay," Ashley said again, still wondering what would happen if she refused one of his suggestions—his orders, really. Was it because she had been in Tall Oaks for so many months, and somehow now she craved the authority from which she had escaped? Or… was it something about Wes the Navy SEAL? He didn't give his orders the way the guards did. The guards ordered you around for their convenience, but Wes seemed to be telling Ashley what to do for, well, Ashley's own good.

And why did *that* thought—for her own good—send a little shiver up her spine as the door closed behind Wes' enormous, flannel-covered back, where his impossibly broad shoulders seemed to ripple with muscles even beneath the thick fabric? He seemed a cross between a warrior and a lumberjack. Ashley had had boyfriends in Pelham, one of them serious enough that she had had to tell him to knock it off when he tried to put his hand up her shirt, but somehow she had never been able to take them seriously as, well, sex objects. Really, with the exception of a couple of teachers, the guards, and the creepy warden, she had never spent any time at all with adult men who weren't family members.

Most important, it seemed to her right now as she

stripped off the t-shirt and caught the rather embarrassing sight of her trim, naked body in the mirror over Wes' dresser, she had never been in the presence of a man who exuded the kind of authority Wes did: authority that seemed to come both from his life as a SEAL and, more deeply, from an essential goodness and kindness in his nature.

He wanted to take care of her. That scared Ashley a little, because for the first time in her life the feeling of enjoying being taken care of came along with a feeling of, well, sexiness. But she couldn't deny that it also excited her despite the butterflies in her tummy and her heart beating a little faster.

All of this about Wes just made for a distraction, though, she thought ruefully as she put her clothes back on. She would call her parents, and they would take her off Wes' hands. She would probably have to go back to another facility, but she knew her father wouldn't doubt her story. He had moved heaven and earth to get her tried as a juvenile after her little red convertible had slammed into the police car and injured the officer. She felt like she could bear to go back, as long as it was in a place where the warden didn't abuse the inmates.

As she washed her face in the bathroom, she resolved to bring back the Westchester pride. Breakfast, then calling her parents, and then a few hours wait for them to arrive. This part would be over, and she would thank Wes and try to forget the way she felt when he told her what to do.

As soon as she sat down at the little kitchen table, Wes put a mug of coffee in front of her, and then a plate of bacon, eggs, and toast. She started in greedily on the food, while he sat across the table sipping his own coffee, just watching her.

"Now I don't mean to pry," he said, after she had wolfed down her third piece of bacon, "but if there's a cop around here who's treating girls wrong I feel like I should know about it. See if I can do anything."

Ashley looked up from her plate. She hadn't thought

about this part. Could she just say she didn't want to talk about it? Wouldn't he suspect she wasn't telling him something? She sucked her lips into a tight line and reached for the coffee, looking at the plain beige mug and desperately trying to figure out what to say.

"Well," she said, her mouth running on way ahead of her brain, "he's planning on moving soon, and…" This was terrible. Something in Ashley had just decided to lie, even though the most rational part of her knew that she should just stop. Not tell Wes the truth, of course, but… not lie. But her mouth kept going. "…and he lives on the other side of that big valley. I don't even know what the town is called."

What did that even mean? She had been looking at the table and now she looked up at him. He had a patient look in his eyes, but she saw that he knew. He knew everything.

"Ashley Lewis, you're in a lot of trouble," he said.

Ashley felt her face crumple. "Don't make me go back. Please, Wes. Please. I'm not… I made a terrible mistake and I was in an accident and a cop got hurt, and so they sent me to juvie, but I'm not like… I mean…" As she started to tell the truth, she saw the look in his eyes grow softer. It didn't lose its sternness completely, but she could tell that he knew Ashley had started to be honest with him.

"I mean I guess I'm a criminal? But… but I wasn't really trying to run away from Tall Oaks—I just needed to run away from the warden. He… abuses the girls and he was going to abuse me."

The look on Wes' face transformed in an instant into an expression of anger so potent that Ashley quailed back, sure that the anger must be directed at her.

"What did he do?" he said, and Ashley saw immediately that his anger hadn't directed itself at her but rather at the warden.

"He said… he said I had to come to his office and… do stuff. Sex stuff."

"Did you?" Now the tenderness returned and… well, it

almost seemed like he might feel a little *jealous* about her, as if his rage hadn't arisen just because the warden had wanted to abuse *a* girl, but even more because he had wanted to abuse Ashley.

"No," she said, shaking her head. "I ran away. The corporation that's running the facility reduced the number of guards at night. But... the warden made a friend of mine do the sex stuff."

Wes exhaled a long breath through his nostrils, looking into Ashley's eyes. "I don't think you can call your parents," he finally said.

"What?"

"Think about it, Ashley. That's exactly where they're going to be looking for you. You could tell the story about the warden, but even though your parents and I might believe you, from what I've heard about the system they're going to put you right back there and the whole thing will get covered up. No, I think I need to help you get somewhere else, and I can start trying to get an investigation going. I can find a way to contact your folks myself."

Ashley felt her jaw drop. "You'd do all that for me?"

Wes smiled. "I guess so. Long story, but I have this thing about helping pretty girls, I guess you could say."

"But..." Ashley's mouth had started up again, but now her brain seemed to be cooperating with it. "Couldn't I stay here with you? Wouldn't that be less risky?"

"Ashley, I need to go all over the place to get materials and deliver furniture. I can't be worrying about you back here, so close to where you escaped from."

"I could come with you. Stay in the truck, or something. Please, Wes. You're like the first good thing that's happened to me in eighteen months. Don't make me leave!"

His brow furrowed as he considered it. Then his eyes darted up and to the right, as if he were searching for inspiration of some kind. Ashley had put her mug down and now held her hands in front of her, clasped in pleading. Finally he looked straight into her eyes.

"Alright, I'm willing. I can stay put for a few weeks at least and get stuff shipped to me, delay my deliveries, that kind of thing, I guess." Then he raised his hand, though, to stop her cry of joy. "But I need to make something perfectly clear about the way it's going to have to be between us."

CHAPTER FOUR

Ashley's face went from elation to confusion. Wes' courage—a facet of his character that never gave him trouble on the battlefield, or jumping out of a plane—came within a hair's-breadth of failing in the face of telling Ashley she would feel his firm hand.

Dammit, though, this girl clearly needed what Wes knew he could give her, and he refused to hide her here on any other basis.

"I can tell you've got a good heart, Ashley, but I can also tell that even if it was an accident that you ran into the police car, the situation that got you there indicates some trouble."

"Trouble?" There was that drawn-up, hard expression again.

"Trouble. I'm not going to hem and haw. You're a spoiled little rich girl."

She tossed her head and rolled her eyes, unconsciously confirming exactly the problem Wes had just diagnosed.

"That's easy for you to say, since you've clearly never met any other girls from Westchester. Not to mention that I've just spent eighteen months in juvie, and you can't stay spoiled in there. Maybe I was a little spoiled when I went in, but I learned to do what they told me and take what they

gave me."

Ashley's green eyes narrowed as she waited for his response. Her defense seemed rehearsed—as if she'd been working on it for months in juvie, trying it out on herself, and hadn't yet had a chance to deliver it to anyone else.

"No, I've never met your friends," Wes admitted. "I can easily believe they're five times as spoiled as you are. But that doesn't mean that you're *not* spoiled, young lady."

"Young lady? What the fuck?"

Wes shook his head. "That's a place to start. You're going to speak like a lady while you're here with me."

"Lady? Young lady? What the actual fuck?"

Well, at least he had succeeded in bringing out her bratty side so fully she wouldn't be able to deny she had defied him. Also, as he provoked this oppositional behavior, his misgivings about the wisdom of initiating her into a disciplinary dynamic had faded quickly away. Ashley Lewis would have a trip over his knee very soon indeed, and he imagined she wouldn't be quite so defiant afterward.

He spoke patiently. "We can talk about the disrespectful way you're addressing me in a few moments. Right now, it's a distraction."

Ashley managed to develop a crease in her brow and widen her eyes at the same time at these words. The effect seemed to Wes oddly adorable, but he refused to brook even that distraction, as pleasant as it was, though he filed the realization that he might be falling for her away for later consideration.

"Distraction?"

"Yes. The fundamental issue is that you're a spoiled brat, and I'm still willing to take you in until we can figure out the best way to handle your situation."

Her face softened a little. She said, "But…"

He nodded. "But. But I'm not going to take you in without making you change your behavior. Teaching you to make better choices."

Ashley tossed her head again, and actually snorted this

time.

"Like right now. You chose to respond to what I said with disrespect."

She looked at him, clearly expecting him to go on and thus relieve her of the need to think about what she had just done with the snort and the toss of the head. Wes merely gazed back into her eyes, thinking that really the scrape on her cheek made her look interestingly dangerous—as well as making him want to take care of her.

"Well?" she finally said.

"Are you going to deny that you chose to respond disrespectfully?"

"This is crazy! I mean... for it to be disrespectful... I mean, I'd have to, like..."

She couldn't untangle it, but at least Wes could see that she had started to try.

"You'd have to admit that the man who took you in and let you lie to him and cleaned your wounds and gave you breakfast deserved your respect. And that's before we even talk about the agreement we're about to make, in which you're going to promise to be respectful, and let me guide you in making good choices."

Ashley's jaw hung open. "*Obey* you, you mean?" she whispered incredulously.

"If you want to think of it like that. I prefer to think of it as respecting my judgment. If I ask you to do something you may ask me why, and you may respectfully state your reasons for thinking you should be allowed to make a different choice. But if I tell you that you still have to do it, you will do it."

"Because you said so?" The crease returned, but now with narrowed eyes. Not quite as adorable, but Wes thought he could get used to it.

"Yes," he said firmly. "And if you ask me why I've told you to do something, and I simply say *Because I said so*, you will do that thing."

The most important question hung in the air now,

palpably, like a moth circling a bare lightbulb. He saw it in Ashley's eyes, and knew she didn't think it had to be asked. Consequences in prison were both harsh and, in Wes' view, entirely unhelpful. Ashley definitely wanted to know what the consequences in Wes' cabin would be, for failing to respect his judgment, but she clearly felt sure that the answer would simply be that Wes would turn her out of his home. That would be the kind of consequence a prison mindset encouraged: the prison equivalent of throwing Ashley out of his cabin would be isolation, a disciplinary measure that didn't actually provide any real discipline at all.

"I also need to tell you," he said gently, "what will happen if you don't respect me."

The crease in her brow deepened. "You'll turn me in, right?"

"No." Wes shook his head. "I don't believe in that kind of discipline."

Ashley's eyes went so wide that the crease disappeared completely. "*Discipline?* Who said anything about *discipline?*"

"Actually," Wes said, "we've been talking about discipline this whole time. Discipline is simply teaching someone to respect her boundaries and other people's boundaries. Turning you in wouldn't set good boundaries, and it wouldn't teach you anything."

In her eyes Wes could see that, as he had suspected it might, the word *discipline* had a special, hidden meaning for her. Ashley was indeed thinking of what he meant, but hoping with at least half her heart that she had got it wrong. She shook her head slightly, perhaps unconsciously.

"In a word, Ashley, I believe in *old-fashioned* discipline for young women."

A startled little noise escaped her, like the tiny yelp of a puppy. The shaking of her head became clearly conscious and more pronounced.

"I may as well say," Wes continued, "that for spoiled brats I also believe in returning a girl to younger way of life. You grew up without a firm hand to guide you. To help you

learn, you're going to become a little girl—a little lady—again, here in my house. You will respect me as your daddy, and call me *daddy* or *sir*, the way a well brought up young lady does."

Ashley's mouth hung open again. Could Wes hear that her breathing had quickened slightly?

"And, Ashley, can you tell me what happens to little ladies who misbehave?"

Her head had poised mid-shake as Wes delivered the news about the younger way of life, but now it shook violently again.

"I'm completely sure, young lady, that you do know. You've already earned your first consequences for the lying and the disrespect, but I'm sure you don't want to make it worse by pretending you don't know what I'm talking about."

"Please, no," she whispered.

"Call me *sir*," Wesley said sternly. "I won't make you call me *daddy* until you're ready."

"Please... sir... no. I can... I mean, like, I'll do what you tell me. I promise."

"I hope you will, honey. But you have to decide right now whether you're going to agree to my conditions. If you do choose to stay, you're going to have your first spanking right after you make this decision. I'll send you into the bedroom to think about it and, if you decide to stay, you'll get changed for your punishment, then come back out here and I'll take you over my knee."

"Can't we... I mean, can't we..." Ashley swallowed hard, clearly fighting for composure. "Can't we say that I'll, you know, do what you say from now on, and we can, like, start now?"

Wes looked back at her levelly. "No."

Her face crumpled. "Please, sir!" Her hands clenched and unclenched in little fists.

Wes couldn't resist: he reached out his own right hand and opened it, took her left gently inside. "I know you're

scared, honey. Have you ever been spanked before, at home?"

She shook her head as a tear trickled down her cheek. Wes could already tell that the very idea of being held accountable this way had started to produce beneficial effects.

"Well, it's going to hurt, and you're going to be one sorry little girl, but I promise it's going to make you feel better afterward."

Ashley bit her lip. "How?"

"You'll feel more secure, knowing you have real boundaries now. That's the way discipline works. The threat can't do it all on its own, especially when you've already lied to me and used bad language. I have to make it completely clear to you that while you're with me you will make better choices about your behavior, or you will pay the price, on your bare bottom."

Her eyes went wide again. "Bare? No. Forget it."

"Bare-bottom discipline is what young ladies get when they're disrespectful, in an old-fashioned home. Knowing that your daddy won't hesitate to take down your panties to punish you will make you think twice about your conduct from here on in."

"But…"

"There are no buts about this, Ashley, except the one that's going to be bare when you go over my knee." Wes spoke sternly now. "Go ahead back into the bedroom. Put on my t-shirt again, with nothing under it. I'll be waiting for you in the living room to spank you."

She had lowered her eyes to her hand, held in his.

"Unless," Wes continued, knowing he needed to offer her a real alternative, "you want to take your chances on your own. I'll drive you to a gas station, and you can call your parents."

She looked up at him sharply. She tried to pull her hand away but Wes held it for a moment, looking into her eyes, before he let it drop. When he did, though, she didn't

withdraw it fully, but left it there, next to her plate on the table, as if in hope that he would take it again in his.

She said very softly, "Does it really have to be on my bare bottom?"

Wes thought he could hear in her words that a reluctant fascination with the idea had begun to take hold. Ashley spoke as if she almost wanted him to say what he did indeed say.

"Yes, honey, I have to punish you that way. And if you're very disrespectful, you'll get an old-fashioned switching."

"A what?" she asked in horror.

"A switching, honey. You'll have to go out into the woods and cut a branch and bring it to me so I can whip you with it. It's the old-fashioned way to make sure a girl remembers her manners."

"You wouldn't really do that, would you?" she pleaded.

"I would only switch you if you really needed it, but, yes, I would. A girl who's had a switching has a sore bottom to remind her for a few days, and sometimes that's what it takes."

Now Ashley was definitely breathing a good deal harder.

"Time to get changed. If you're going to stay, I want you back here in the t-shirt, ready for your spanking. If not, you can go ahead and come back wearing your own clothes. You can take as long as you want to make up your mind."

CHAPTER FIVE

Ashley stayed in the bedroom, looking at Wes' t-shirt, for a long time. What her mind couldn't seem to get past was the difference between the horrible thing the warden had said about the paddle in his office, about how he didn't mind tanning a girl's hide, and what Wes had said.

Nothing in her heart or head had felt the slightest fascination or interest in bending over the warden's desk so that he could take down her underwear and swat her with a wooden thing that had holes to make it hit harder. Nothing.

But... Wes. *Take you over my knee.*

She didn't want it. No, of course she didn't want it.

But she did want to stay with him, and the things he said about discipline... if you took away the spanking, and the fear of the spanking, Ashley had to admit that she couldn't argue with him in good faith. She *was* spoiled. If she hadn't been so spoiled, she probably wouldn't have been at the party, doing the underage drinking that all her spoiled friends did. She wouldn't have crashed into the police car, and she wouldn't have found herself sent to Tall Oaks.

In juvie, that spoiled part of her had become her defense against the horrors of the place: Westchester pride, seeing her through. Acting respectful enough to get by, but not

really respectful. Certainly not respectful the way it seemed Wes had decided he would try to get Ashley to act. She had come to the conclusion, without doing any reasoning along the way, that she had formed her character—no, that Tall Oaks had formed her character. For better or worse, she had her pride, and she would keep it even after she left juvie. The world had done her an injustice in return for a youthful mistake with the drinking and driving, and Ashley Lewis would face the world with disdain and a hardened exterior that could see her through.

She would be a spoiled brat forever.

Ashley gazed down at the t-shirt, which had the name of what might be Wes' college on the breast, though she didn't recognize the name. He probably came from the Midwest and had gone to one of *those* colleges. But he had gone to college—she could tell, even if the t-shirt were somehow not from his own college, or not from a college at all. Ashley didn't think all Navy SEALs went to college, but she knew a lot of them did, and more important, the way Wes spoke demonstrated absolutely that despite the rough-hewn appearance and the homemade furniture, he had had a good education even by the standards of Westchester.

Over my knee. Why the hell was she thinking about his education when the choice in front of her, whether to put on the t-shirt—with no panties—or simply walk out of the room and out of his life as she was, demanded making. He had said she could have as much time as she needed. Suddenly she wished he hadn't said that, wished he had said she could have five minutes, wished those five minutes were up now, and he was opening the door without knocking, telling her that if she wouldn't put on the t-shirt he would just take down her jeans and panties right there and give her the bare-bottom discipline she needed without further ceremony.

Did she want to make sure the man who spanked her when she misbehaved—who planned to treat her like a little girl in order to bring her back up properly—had the

necessary academic credentials? Despite everything, the thought made her smile.

She had no choice, though, really, did she? She would never find another person to help her, or a better place to hide. Strange as it seemed, facing her first spanking by a man she had known for only a few hours, Ashley knew how lucky she had gotten. Trying not to think about what would happen when she returned to the living room, she started to tug her own blue t-shirt over her head.

Ashley took off her panties last, after she had dropped Wes' much bigger shirt over her head. She faced the door to the living room for a few seconds, trying to work up the courage to shed her last vestige of pride. How could she, of her own free will, pull down her own underwear in order that a man could punish her the way naughty little girls are punished? To have to get ready for her spanking, and acknowledge Wes' right to discipline her the old-fashioned way, seemed at that moment a terrible loss of everything Ashley had tried to hold onto so tightly for the last eighteen months.

It would hurt so much. Wes' hand, grasping hers gently at the table, seemed the size of a dinner plate. And he would pull up the t-shirt now and bring that hand down so hard on her poor bottom. Over and over, until Ashley couldn't sit down, because she had behaved badly and gotten what she deserved.

She turned from the door, as if she didn't want him to see her taking off her panties through the door somehow, from the front where he might catch a little flash of something he shouldn't see. Something he *definitely* shouldn't see, because... well, he shouldn't.

She reached under the t-shirt and hooked her thumbs into the waistband. They came down in a tangle over her hips, and she stepped awkwardly out of them. She laid them on the bed and turned quickly away toward the door.

When she emerged into the living room, she found Wes sitting on a sturdy straight-backed wooden chair that he had

set in the middle of the room, directly across from the bedroom door. *No arms*, she thought. *So I can lay myself over his lap.*

He looked straight into Ashley's eyes and patted his right thigh. "Come here, young lady," he said surprisingly gently. "Stand next to me here, and then lay yourself down for your spanking."

Ashley took a step forward and then froze. An emotion she hadn't expected rose in her chest: supplication—hope that the person in charge might hear a plea for mercy.

"Please, sir," she said in a soft voice she hadn't even known she possessed. "It's my first time."

Wes smiled in a kind, caring way whose effect on her took her by surprise. She felt her mouth turn up in a classic little-girl pout, and her heart started to beat very fast.

"I know, honey," he said in the same gentle voice. "I need to teach you your lesson, but I promise that I won't punish you more severely than will help you behave yourself. I'm going to turn your backside a nice bright red, because that's what you earned, but once we have this first punishment out of the way I think you'll understand much better why I'm taking you in hand like this."

Taking you in hand. Ashley swallowed hard, breathed in and out with two short pants, started to move forward in tiny steps.

"Hurry up, honey," Wes said. "Let's get this over with. Over my lap like a good girl, now."

He patted his thigh again. Ashley tried to speed up, but her body didn't want to obey her. She had never felt anything like the mix of dread and hope that now seemed to course through her body, making her knees grow weak and her heart race.

Wes didn't speak again, but left her to move, unable now to meet his eyes, to his right side. She looked down at his enormous, sinewy thighs, covered in faded denim. How could she lay herself down of her own volition?

He helped her, though. She jumped as she felt his arm

around her waist, but she felt grateful, too, for this little bit of guidance: he tugged, and she did bend, did feel her own thighs, scantily clad in the thin cotton of the t-shirt, come up against his.

"Reach forward and take the legs of the chair in your hands, Ashley," he said, and now she could feel the way his deep voice seemed to make his whole body and even the chair itself rumble. "That will help you keep your butt nice and high for me."

"What?" she whispered, truly mystified as to what he meant. She remained just slightly bent over, with Wes' arm still around her waist.

"A girl who's being punished needs to present her backside respectfully to her daddy. That shows she understands he's spanking her for her own good."

Ashley bit her lip. The notion seemed to make sense on some level, but her mind rebelled against it.

"Ashley," Wes said, his voice becoming a little stern. "Do as I said. Reach forward and lay yourself down. I don't want to have to hold you down while I spank you."

"Oh, God," she whispered. "Please, sir. Please." But even as she whispered these words she had begun to reach forward and bend further.

"Good girl," Wes said approvingly. Ashley's heart jumped at the warmer tone in his voice. But even as he said the reassuring words he used the hand around her waist to urge her further over, upend her completely so that she was on tiptoe, her bottom indeed raised up over his right thigh. And she did need to present her rear like that, lifted, because otherwise her front would rub up against his leg. She felt her face turning crimson at the thought, and she kept her knees tightly together. She gripped the legs of the chair, trying to take comfort from their solidity and from the way holding them tightly represented her obedience to Wes: he would see that she could obey him, and maybe he wouldn't spank her as hard.

His left arm now came down across her waist. "Don't

let go of the chair, honey," he said. "If you think about that you won't be tempted to try to put your hand back to cover your bottom. You must never try to do that, or you'll get extra. When I spank you, your bottom is mine to punish, and it's very disrespectful to interfere. I know you don't understand completely right now, but do you think you see what I'm saying?"

Ashley's breath came so fast she thought she might faint. "Yes, sir," she whispered.

He put his hand there, then: his huge right hand, behind her where she couldn't see, above her because he had taken her over his knee for old-fashioned discipline, on her bottom, holding her little cheeks through the thin fabric of his t-shirt.

"This part of you," he said with a kind of solemnity that made Ashley's heart beat even faster, "is the place where you will receive correction, in my house." Then she gasped, because he had raised the hem of the t-shirt, and he could see her bare backside now. "When I uncover your little butt, Ashley, to teach you a lesson, I want you to remember that I will only discipline you to help you learn, and to guide you to become a better and happier person."

He paused, and she knew she must speak again. "Yes, sir."

He put his hand on her bare bottom, then, as he had put it there a moment before when it had still lain hidden by the red cotton. Ashley gasped as he squeezed her there, very gently. At that moment, something that had hidden itself up until his touching her bare skin, seemed to break out inside her. *Oh, no*, she thought, as a warmth seemed to spread forward from his palm and the pressure of his fingers.

"You lied, and you disrespected me, young lady. Now you're going to find out what happens to naughty girls in my house. This butt is going to feel my firm hand as often as necessary, until you can behave yourself like the little lady you know you can be."

CHAPTER SIX

Wes had spanked two other girls before Ashley Lewis. His college girlfriend Julie had come from a Southern family where the punishment of adult women formed an accepted part of family life. When she had gotten much too drunk one night, and he had told her the next morning that she had to clean up her act, she had bitten her lip and confessed that she knew he would have to spank her.

"Please, just over my panties," Julie said. "Not on the bare, please, Wes?"

Wes had the knack of sizing up situations very quickly and almost always identifying the best available option.

"Do you get spanked on the bare at home?" he asked, fascinated and rather turned on.

Julie nodded as a furrow appeared on her brow.

"Well, I think you'll need to take your panties down for me, then. In fact, I think I need you to take off all your clothes for your punishment."

Spanking Julie that morning, and several more times in the two years they had dated, had taught him about the connection between discipline and sex that existed for him and at least for some women. Julie always obeyed him readily, if with a blush, when he told her to take her clothes

off for punishment, even when Wes trumped up a reason, like the time he spanked her for getting a C on a test, and she always got wet between her legs as soon as he stopped spanking her and began to soothe her warm, red bottom.

After that first spanking, and then each subsequent time, Wes laid Julie on the bed on her tummy and fucked her very hard from behind. His senses overcome with the arousal of spanking his naked girlfriend and hearing her cry out so ambiguously as he punished her, then realizing her shaved pussy had gotten as warm as her bottom, he let his dominant instincts take over. He said nothing, but simply put Julie into the posture he wanted, with her knees spread and her pink cunt visibly glistening. He took off his jeans and got on the bed, crouching over her, and entered that soaking wet cunt as Julie cried out. He thrust in and out with abandon, and that was when Julie helped him discover ageplay, because she started to moan, "Oh, daddy. Please. Please, daddy. I'll be so good. My little cunt is so wet, daddy, because you know how to spank me and fuck me like this."

He had spanked his next girlfriend, Angela, too, but only for discipline, and without a daddy/little-girl dynamic in their relationship. They hadn't dated long, and Wes suspected that Angela lied to him when he asked her after the first spanking, which he had given her for being an hour late for their third date, whether the punishment aroused her. She had said, "Of course not," but when they had sex later that night—Wes had marched her out of the restaurant and spanked her in his car—Angela had wriggled her heart-shaped backside so provocatively that he had wondered if she meant it as an invitation. Sure enough, when he said, "I want to fuck you in the ass," Angela said, a bit nervously, "Okay," and Wes got to sample for the first time the heady pleasures of a tight little anus around his driving cock.

They were together for four months, right before Wes deployed overseas, and he only spanked her two or three more times, for example after she mouthed off about one of his friends and refused to apologize. He had the urge to

treat Angela as a naughty little girl, but he could tell that though she did respond reasonably well to discipline, she didn't have the little side of her nature that Julie had, and that Marmara had. That Ashley Lewis seemed pretty clearly to have, too.

He did take Angela anally several more times, too, but neither that bottom sex nor anything else they did in the bedroom had any explicit connection to the spanking. Angela seemed to like having a boyfriend who wouldn't hesitate to punish her when she got out of line, but she didn't seem to like to think about it too hard. When Wes carelessly told her in front of one of her girlfriends that Angela had a spanking coming later, and the friend had asked in fascination whether he meant it, Angela had said, "Of course not," though her bright red cheeks betrayed her. Wes had spanked her harder for lying to her friend, and part of him wanted to instruct Angela that she must tell her friend that Wes did indeed spank her bare bottom regularly, but he had already received his orders, and it was clear that he and Angela would break up soon.

So even if Ashley got aroused by her punishment, Wes knew how to keep the discipline separate from any sex or romance that might develop. He would know soon enough, he imagined, whether she might want to be his little girl in more ways than simply the disciplinary. For now he needed to make it clear that when he gave a punishment he would make it a real lesson, no matter how distracting her taut little cheeks felt in his hand.

He lifted that hand high and brought it down hard. Wes always spanked quickly and forcefully, to make the nature of the occasion clear to the girl he was disciplining. Spank followed spank, and Ashley cried out and started to struggle over Wes' lap. She kicked, showing a hint of her furry little pussy that Wes refused to look at too closely as he kept spanking her.

"Sir... oh, please... it hurts so much!"

Wes held her firmly around her waist with his left hand

and continued bringing his hand down hard on the little bottom that had already turned a light pink. Ashley wailed, and kicked again.

"Stop kicking this minute, young lady," he said sternly. "Learn right now to take your spanking the way a good girl does."

But now she had thrown her right hand behind her, and he had to seize her wrist in his left hand to hold it fast. She kicked again, and now Wes shifted her as easily as he might move a bag of flour so that he could trap her legs between his own.

"Please, no," Ashley sobbed as she felt how Wes had immobilized her.

"We're almost done, honey," Wes said. "But I have to keep your bottom still so I can punish you the way you need." He started in again, spanking the rosy cheeks that lay now entirely at his disposal. The will to struggle seemed to go out of Ashley and she lay limp over his knee, yelping at each hard spank, but also, Wes thought, even trying to keep her bottom well presented for him, the cheeks clenching and unclenching as she tried in vain to soothe the smart.

He gave her three more swats, and then he put his hand there softly and began to rub the warm little cheeks, ignoring as best he could how hard his cock had gotten. Even with Julie, he had never been so turned on just giving a spanking. He had an instinctive, gut-level feeling that Ashley wanted him as much as he wanted her, but Wes refused to take advantage of her helplessness right after this punishment. He needed to be sure.

He got a good deal more sure when he heard the way Ashley moaned as he made gentle circles with his fingers, and though he had no trouble denying himself the pleasure of trying her arousal with a fingertip dipped naughtily between her thighs, he could smell quite clearly now that wonderful wicked scent of a young pussy in need of masculine attention.

"Are you going to behave respectfully from now on,

young lady?" he asked softly.

"Yes, sir," Ashley half moaned and half sobbed.

Wes smoothed the t-shirt back down over her bottom, which was now almost as red as the scarlet cotton. A pang of regret at losing the sexy view went through him, but he found more than ample compensation in gathering Ashley up into his arms and snuggling her against his chest, especially because she made a wonderful little cooing sound when she felt what he was doing.

She nestled her face against his flannel shirt, and for a moment she seemed to cry even harder, as if his tenderness after the strict lesson he had taught her made even clearer her need for repentance. She heaved only two sobs, though, and then she lay still in his arms. Wes didn't think he had ever felt anything so heavenly. The simple smallness of Ashley's body, and the contrast of her little-girl cuddliness with her grownup needs made him want to sit like that with her forever, just making sure she knew that now that she had promised to follow his rules he considered himself a very lucky daddy—whether or not he got to do anything about how aroused the spanking seemed to have gotten her.

"Thank me for spanking you, Ashley," he said softly. Wes considered it an important part of the lesson.

"What?" Ashley said distractedly and a little bewildered.

"You need to thank me for teaching you your lesson. Even if you're not really feeling grateful, I want you to work on understanding that I discipline you for your own good." He rested his chin atop her still tangled hair, which nevertheless smelled good to him: lingering shampoo plus the scents of the forest.

"Oh," she said, snuggling in a little closer. "Thank you, sir. I… I do feel, you know, a little grateful. Now that I have it over with. It's like a have a clean slate now, or something."

"Exactly, honey. That's exactly it."

He could sit there forever, but he had to move things along if they were going to understand each other fully, and his cock felt so hard under her little bottom that, as delicious

as the cuddling was, he had to admit to a little discomfort.

"Alright. I need to make sure you don't have any scrapes I didn't see before, honey."

"What?" Ashley spoke a little dreamily now.

"I'm going to give you a bath."

"But... my hair... I need a shower."

"You can finish up with a shower, after I clean the rest of you."

It seemed like a good way to stay near her, as well as to make clear how seriously he took his responsibility to take care of her. And of course it would let her try out what it felt like to have a daddy who claimed the privilege of inspecting and washing every part of her young body, even if this time—and perhaps in the future—he stayed away from the naughtier bits.

He rose from the chair with Ashley still in his arms and carried her to the couch, where he lowered her gently onto the cushions. "You stay here, honey, while I draw the bath."

"Okay, sir," Ashley whispered. Her eyes had gotten very wide, as if the thought of being bathed by a man who had just spanked her had taken her completely aback, though Wes thought he could tell that she felt no fear, but only wonder and—maybe, judging by her breathing—arousal.

Wes went to the little bathroom, in which he had nevertheless installed a very big tub. He didn't think of his fondness for baths as a weakness, but he had to admit that he had been a little extravagant with the gleaming white tub and shower enclosure. On the other hand, he had really wanted to blow a good chunk of his savings on a whirlpool tub, but had managed to restrain himself.

A big man needs a big tub. If taking a bath *alongside* Ashley were in his future, or even with Ashley *atop* him—he couldn't help considering, with a little leap of his cock—he would be very glad indeed that he hadn't skimped on the size.

CHAPTER SEVEN

Could she let this happen? Wes the Navy SEAL bathing her, with no clothes on, in that enormous tub she had seen when she peed that morning?

He had just *spanked* her. And now he said he was going to wash her, in the bathtub, as if she were the young lady, the little girl, he kept talking about.

Was Ashley Lewis that young lady? Until fifteen minutes ago she would never in her wildest dreams have imagined that her body would respond the way it had to him. But his sheer *bigness*, and his experience—they seemed to work on her senses like an intoxicant, until she couldn't even recognize the facts about her that she had always thought defined her. Like who her boyfriends would be.

She had never thought about sex much, even when the warden had promised to make her do sex things. That was just about power.

Wasn't *this* about power, too, though? But power used for good as opposed to power used for evil?

Wes came back. Ashley could hear the water running into the tub now.

She spoke without really thinking about it, not even sure what answer she wanted. "Can I keep the t-shirt on in the

tub, sir? I mean, you know, to… cover me?"

Wes smiled patiently as she looked up at him from the couch.

"No, honey. You have to take it off so I can see all of you. I'll go get new clothes for you and let you use the washcloth on your privates, once I'm done with the rest of you."

She felt her face go very red. How could he just say that about her *privates*? And her privates were so… well, they had gotten so warm and even wet, at the beginning of the spanking and then when he rubbed her bottom, and even when he had snuggled her in his arms. She had felt that kind of warmth before only a couple of times—never with a boyfriend, but just lying in bed thinking about things, like certain movie stars and certain movies.

Ashley knew theoretically that it was possible to use your hand to soothe that warmth away, but she never had, feeling always that to do that would be to give in to the feeling in some way, and thinking that she didn't want to be the kind of girl who gave in that way.

Now, though, the urge to put her hand down there, between her thighs, on her privates—even with Wes *watching*—started to grow way, way past any point to which it had ever come before. To have him say *privates* seemed to light a fire in the place he named, so great that the warmth began to turn into an ache.

Wes bent down and picked her up just as easily as he had maneuvered her over his knee during the spanking, at that terrible moment when he had rendered her bottom completely motionless so he could finish punishing it. The worst part of the spanking had turned out not to be the pain, which did become bad, but the way being over Wes' lap had made the pain somehow connect to her soul, so that to keep her bottom pushed up the way he wanted it became its own lesson in obeying him, and she really did feel ashamed that she couldn't keep herself from kicking and couldn't keep her right hand from trying to cover her poor little bottom.

The best part, of course, was when he took her in his arms, as she was in his arms now. To feel that she had had her first bare-bottom spanking, to teach her how she must behave from now on, and that the man who gave it to her—who had taken her in hand—wanted to hold her that way... well, it made being carried into the bathroom feel even more like flying than it already did.

The water was warm and bubbly. She didn't think hard about why a former special ops warrior living in a cabin in the woods should have bubble bath, but merely enjoyed the perfectly warm temperature of the bath as, after standing up briefly so Wes could strip the t-shirt off her, she scrambled into the tub, wanting him to get as brief a glimpse as possible of her pussy.

Had he seen it when she kicked, during the spanking? At the time, she had been in too much discomfort even to think about it, but now she felt another blush suffuse her face. She looked down; the bubbles covered her up, thank goodness. But Wes handed her a washcloth and said, "You can put this down there to cover your privates if you want."

She smiled nervously up at him. "Thanks," she said as she took it and submerged it there. Somehow, though, to have the washcloth there made the feeling that, as strange as it seemed, she *wanted* Wes to see her pussy even stronger. She swallowed hard.

Wes had turned away to get another washcloth, and now he dipped it in the sudsy water and began gently to wash her face. The scrape on her cheek, though far from completely healed, hurt a lot less than it had only a few hours before. The warm cloth on her face felt delicious, and when Wes moved to her shoulders and upper arms, Ashley realized that she had started to press down on the washcloth between her thighs, and the ache there was growing. Oh, God, was she actually masturbating here in front of him? She guiltily eased the pressure, though her pussy seemed to cry out for more.

If Wes noticed anything unusual, he didn't mention it.

Just brushing against her breasts, he moved down to her tummy, clearly working to make sure he didn't tickle her by making each sweep of the cloth even and long.

"Lean forward, honey," he said, "and I'll wash your back."

Then it was her thighs, inches away from where Ashley held the washcloth, her calves, and her feet.

Then he said, "Alright, I'll go find some clothes. You finish up. Wash your privates and then you can drain the tub and take a shower."

He left the bathroom, the door behind him remaining ajar.

Ashley nearly refrained even from trying to wash herself between her legs, but how could she? The merest touch of the washcloth, though, as she spread her legs in the spacious tub and began to rub there, sent a shudder of terrible pleasure through her whole body. She had never felt arousal this strong. Suddenly the need to see Wes naked, the way he had seen her, seemed to take command of her imagination. She had never seen a man's penis outside a picture in sex-ed class, but now she couldn't stop picturing Wes', hard and ready to do the thing Ashley had of course known she would do one day but had never really considered in relation to an actual, individual man. Sex. *Fucking*. For the very first time, Ashley Lewis thought she would like to be fucked, with a hard cock thrusting into her tender little privates. Wes' hard cock.

She had her fingers under the washcloth now. She was playing with herself, not washing herself; how could she deny it? If Wes fucked her with his hard cock, it would go in *here*, where she could feel the opening, very low down. Two fingers could get in, and make her moan, while with the other hand she rubbed the place at the top with the dirty, dirty name: *clitoris*. *Clit*.

Would Wes spank her for masturbating? The very thought made the arousal fiercer, worse and better. The two fingers could go in a little way, but then they came up against

what she knew must be her hymen—with too much force.

Ashley cried out in startled discomfort.

Wes came in, holding a t-shirt and athletic shorts, a concerned look on his face. In his eyes, she saw him realize exactly what was going on.

"Would you like daddy to do that for you, honey?" he asked softly. "Your daddy is the one who should make you feel good that way. Little girls who touch themselves without permission get spanked, because their daddies are in charge of their privates. I know you didn't know that, though, so I'm not going to spank you."

"B-but…" Ashley stammered, so embarrassed and so aroused that she wasn't even sure she wasn't about to ask him to spank her anyway.

"But now you do know that rule, and you either have to stop touching yourself, or tell daddy that you would like him to be the one to play with your little pussy."

Ashley stared back at him, trying to make sense of the choice he offered her. Could he actually be saying that he would punish her for what she wanted to do with her own body, if she refused to let him touch her that way? As much arousal as she felt, something about that idea seemed wrong to her.

As if reading her mind, Wes said, in a very different kind of voice. "Ashley, I'm asking you if you want to start what's called an ageplay relationship with me. If you decide you *don't* want me to be your daddy, that's fine, and I won't spank you for masturbating. That's part of the ageplay dynamic, and if you don't want that dynamic I'll just turn around and go, and this time I'll shut the door behind me." The ghost of a smile appeared on his lips, and it reassured her greatly.

"N-no…" she said, realizing that her hands had remained in the embarrassing places they had been when he walked in; now she guiltily moved them away and replaced the washcloth between her thighs.

"No, what?" Wes asked softly.

"No, daddy?"

His little smile turned into a grin. "That's not what I meant, but I think I can tell what you mean."

Ashley couldn't help smiling back, as terribly strange as the whole situation seemed.

"No, don't go?" she whispered.

"You want your daddy to make your little pussy feel good?"

"Yes, daddy," she said, even more softly. "Please, daddy."

"Did my little girl's pussy get wet when she had her spanking?"

Why did it feel so perfect? So much better than anything had ever felt, to have this man only, what, maybe seven years older than she was, calling her a little girl and saying such dirty, naughty things to her. She could only think that Wes had been right: she needed a kind of discipline she would never have thought she could find, now that she had, according to the way most of the world looked at it, grown far past it.

"Yes, daddy. It got so wet, and I couldn't help it. I had to touch it."

Wes crossed the few steps so he could bend down and reach into the tub—deep into the tub, down between her legs. Ashley moaned so loud as he touched her there, began to rub her there with fingers that seemed to know how to soothe the aching and the burning, even better than she could herself knew.

"You won't always be allowed to have your pussy touched after a spanking," he said right in her ear, as his fingers made her back arch and her hands ball into fists. "When you've been naughty, sometimes daddy will need to make sure you understand that only good girls get to come."

Ashley's mouth hung open, her breath coming in short pants. She felt sweat beading on her brow. *Come.* She knew that some women couldn't have orgasms, and she had thought she might be one of them. Wes was teaching her a

new lesson, now: Ashley Lewis no longer doubted that she could come. The question would be whether she could be a good enough girl to come several times every day, the way her delirious brain seemed to be telling her she could never live without, because *this*, now, with her whole body spasming and splashing in the bubbly warm water, with Wes' enormous hand still caressing her mercilessly, gently, *this* must be what coming was.

CHAPTER EIGHT

After the tension started to leave her body, Wes kept his hand on Ashley's furry pussy possessively, still fondling but not actively wanking his wonderful little girl.

"Did that feel good, honey?" he asked.

"Yes, daddy," Ashley whispered.

"Would you like daddy to help you in the shower?"

She giggled: a wonderful silvery sound that seemed to shine light into places in Wes that had been dark for two years.

"Yes, daddy. You'd have to take off your clothes, wouldn't you?"

"Would you like to see your daddy naked, honey? Have you ever seen a naked man?"

"Only in pictures," Ashley said with another giggle.

"So you've never seen a man's penis up close?"

"Oh, daddy!" She tucked her chin into her shoulder as pink spread across her face.

"I know it's a little embarrassing," Wes said, smiling, "but a little girl who touches herself in the bathtub is ready to have big-girl time, and that means learning to make her daddy's penis get hard, and learning to make it feel good until the semen comes out. After your shower, daddy's

going to put his penis inside your little pussy."

He rubbed her there again, and her whole body quaked with the pleasure of the touch and, he felt sure, the dirty talk that he loved so much. Her face had turned bright crimson now.

"And we're going to shave you down here, too," he said, not wanting to stop the flow of her arousal, or his—Wes' cock felt like an iron bar inside his jeans and delaying taking them off and feeling Ashley's first tentative attentions to her daddy's pleasure had become a delicious torment.

"Oh, no…" Ashley said, as Wes began to run his fingers more pointedly up and down her tender slit, moving her toward another orgasm.

"Yes, honey. A daddy likes to have a smooth place to put his cock, so that when he looks down at what he's doing he can see himself moving inside her. And a little girl likes to have a tidy private place under her panties, so she can always feel nice and clean. We'll get you shaved tomorrow: daddy can't wait much longer to fuck you."

At the coarse, grown-up word, Ashley shuddered with pleasure and cried out over his fingers. Wes could tell she loved dirty talk just as much as he did.

"Move against daddy's hand, honey. Help him make his little girl come. When daddy gives you permission, you can be as naughty as you want with your little pussy."

She needed no further urging, but began to move her hips in the water, shamelessly bucking them so that she could rub her clit on his fingers even as they fondled her there.

"That's it, honey. Such a good girl to show your daddy how much you need his big cock inside you."

"Oh, God. Oh, God." Ashley's voice sounded strangled, as if this orgasm was going to be much bigger than the first; so big that she felt like her body couldn't even deal with the pleasure.

"Come for daddy, now, and then daddy will show you his penis," he whispered in her ear, and that set her off: she

cried out and splashed water out of the tub and onto Wes' jeans with the arching of her back that seemed to go on forever.

"You got daddy wet, honey," Wes said in mock reproach. Now he didn't spend any time soothing her pussy, because his need had become simply too great. He stood up, unbuttoning his flannel shirt. He stripped off his jeans, so that his cock sprang free right in front of Ashley's face where she sat in the tub.

She gave a little moaning gasp. "Oh, daddy," she whispered. "It's too big. Isn't it? It won't fit inside me!"

"Shh," Wes said, holding the hard length of his manhood in his right hand and pumping it gently as he looked at his naked little girl in her bubble bath. "It will hurt a little, but you'll get used to it. You're going to have it inside you every day from now on. Open your mouth."

"Oh, no. Please. Please, daddy. I don't think… I mean, I'm not ready?"

"Daddy will be gentle, honey, but he needs to be in your pretty mouth right now. Open up for him, so he can make himself feel good the way a daddy likes to do."

Ashley's eyes seemed to glow in response to the dominant tone Wes had instilled in his voice. "Please, daddy," she whispered. "Please don't spank me again."

Wes fought to keep the smile off his face so that the paternal sternness could stay there, turning both of them on. "If you don't want another spanking, Ashley, you need to open those lips right now, and stick out your tongue. You promised to respect my wishes, and I don't think I've ever wished for anything as much as I want to teach you to suck my cock, right now. I won't make you swallow today, but I'm going to claim your face with my semen. I need to come so that when I fuck your pussy for the first time I can be as gentle as I want to be."

Ashley's forehead developed a deep crease and her eyes opened very wide, as if she couldn't believe how turned on the threat of a spanking had made her, now that Wes had

begun to take her in hand sexually as well as for disciplinary purposes. *We're going to have so much fun, crossing this line over and over, little girl*, he thought as he watched her jaw slowly drop and her sweet pink tongue even more slowly extend over her lower lip.

"That's it," he murmured stepping forward, still holding his cock. "Good girl. Good girl. Here you go." He laid the head on her tongue, loving the way it looked and the way it felt to make eighteen-year-old Ashley Lewis suck a penis for the first time. He put his hands gently around the back of her head.

"Daddy's going to fuck your face a little now, honey," he said, and began to move in and out only a few inches. "The next time you do this, I'll teach you how to move your head to make me feel good."

God, it was hard to be gentle: Wes wanted to thrust in deep, make his little girl gag, and shoot his seed into her sweet tummy. But he contented himself with the shallow motion, just loving the way Ashley looked up at him, as if in wonder that she had become such a big girl today.

Close to coming, he pulled out. "Hold it in your hands, honey," he said. "Rub it the way you saw me do, and just kiss the top to show how important daddy's cock is to you. Keep your eyes on daddy's penis so you can learn to give it pleasure."

Giggling a little now, as if at the almost over-the-top dirty talk, she put her hands, wet and soapy from the tub, on the hard length of him, already moist from her mouth. She kissed very sweetly, and kept her eyes obediently lowered. She rubbed, a little clumsily, but Wes couldn't suppress a grunt of pleasure.

"Put one hand under my balls, honey, and just hold them gently. That makes daddy feel very good. That's it. So nice."

Very close now, he moved her left hand away from his cock and pumped his erection himself. Ashley looked up again, seeming a little startled.

"Close your eyes and your mouth, honey," Wes said as

gently as he could. "Daddy is going to give you your first facial."

Her eyes went even wider, and then she shut them tight and pursed her lips. Wes put his right hand down to play with her perfect little breasts, taking their pink nipples in his fingers to make her sigh. He reached down further, and held her virgin cunt, ready for fucking, in his hand, and the thought of fucking her, so very soon, sent him over the edge. His seed spurted out all over Ashley's cheeks and her forehead and her chin, as she gave a startled cry.

"Now, honey," Wes said gently, "you really do need a shower, don't you?"

He kept her warm in his arms while the water drained, enjoying the wonderful feeling of his naked skin against hers, of his cock naughtily touching her bare tummy and making her giggle. When they got into the shower and he pulled the curtain closed, the warm water embracing them together, he turned Ashley around and made her stand in front of him, so that while she washed her hair he could play with the sweet little bottom he had spanked so hard. Wickedly he moved his already re-stiffening cock against the pert, adorable cheeks, parting them and even pushing the head against the secret little ring there, letting her know even before he told her in words that she would have to have his cock there, too, very soon.

"Daddy! What are you doing?" she said, turning her face, scrubbed clean of semen now, over her shoulder to try to look at him. Her hair smelled deliciously of the fruit-scented shampoo and looked sleek and sexy as it twisted over her neck. Wes didn't answer for a moment, but bent down to give her an awkward but very passionate kiss, still pushing his cockhead between her adorable bottom-cheeks as their tongues met gently in the warm, falling water.

"A good little girl takes her daddy's cock wherever he wants to put it," he said, when he broke the kiss at last. "You'll have your first lesson in bottom sex sometime soon, honey."

"But… but why, daddy? Why do you want to put your… you know… in *there*?"

Wes smiled, wondering if Ashley even knew how thoroughly she had started to enter into the ageplay. He moved his hands from her pert backside and took her right breast in his hand, cupping it and thumbing the nipple, while he put his left hand down between her thighs, loving how available his sweet girl's virgin pussy was to him now, and would be from now on. Ashley bit her lip as if at the arousal her daddy forced on her so casually.

He spoke softly. "I want to claim all of you, honey. To fuck your bottom is part of that. I want you to understand that when your daddy wants pleasure from your young body, he'll have it, and you'll learn to be a better girl by giving it to him, even if it hurts a little." Her brow creased as if in fear, but Wes rubbed her clit a little more firmly, and her eyes widened with a little sigh from her throat. "Daddy is in charge of you now, and he's in charge of your anus, too. Because your anus is the most private place of all on your body, and because it's so nice and tight, daddy will spend a lot of time in there, enjoying himself and teaching you your lessons."

"Lessons?" Ashley whispered.

"Are you all clean, honey?" Wes asked.

Ashley nodded.

"Then let's get you dry and into bed. It's time for you to have sex. Then I'll tell you more about your bottom lessons, after I've fucked your pussy for the first time and you know what it's like to have a man's hardness inside you, claiming you."

He reluctantly let go of her breast and reached out to turn the water off. From the hook next to the shower he took a big fluffy white towel and wrapped it around her, kissing her again as he snuggled her up in his arms. She trembled as he held her.

"Why?" she whispered, looking up at him with wide eyes.

"Why what, honey?" Wes asked, smiling.

"Why is it... I mean, how can it be so, you know, wrong... but..."

"So right, too?" He put his hand on her terry-cloth covered backside and squeezed it possessively. Ashley giggled and nestled against him more firmly.

"Oh, daddy," she said, and kissed his chest. Then she whispered, "Daddies shouldn't fuck their little girls' bottoms, should they?"

Wes pulled up the towel so he could hold her bare bottom and work his middle finger inside the crack, touch her there, push in there just a little. Ashley gave a little moaning cry.

"They should if that's what they think their little girls need, honey. Tell me the truth. Do you need your daddy's cock in here?" He moved his fingertip in and out gently. "I'm sure you never knew that's what you needed before now, but if I'm right about my little girl, you're starting to understand your needs a lot better today."

"Yes, daddy," Ashley murmured, and kissed his chest again.

CHAPTER NINE

Wes picked Ashley up and carried her, in the fluffy towel, from the bathroom to the bedroom. He laid her down on the queen-sized bed and pulled the covers off so that she lay on the bare fitted sheet. She looked up at him in surprise; this wasn't what she thought *getting into bed* involved.

"When I fuck you, honey, I don't want any covers to get in the way. I like to look at what I'm doing, and I'm going to move you around the way I want you. Remember who's in charge."

She bit her lip. "Daddy," she said softly.

This transition to suddenly calling him *daddy* still seemed jarring, but at the same time Ashley didn't think she could ever get enough of it—enough of the sense of caring and at the same time the sense of dirtiness. And Wes seemed to want to make her keep thinking about the naughtiest parts.

Like her bottom. She would never have thought that having a man's finger there would feel anything other than embarrassing—and it was indeed terribly embarrassing—but the way he talked to her about what he wanted to do with her, how he wanted to seek his pleasure in every part of her body, seemed to make everything strange and

different. *Did* she need her daddy's cock in her bottom? Ashley wasn't sure... but she couldn't deny, as much as she still would have liked to, that the thought of him making her take his cock there, in her most private place, made her warm between her thighs as she watched him finish drying himself.

His cock: the cock he had put in her mouth and moved in and out for his pleasure. So big, and so hard—and getting hard again, she could see with a blush. Every time she looked at it her face seemed to get hot, but then she couldn't help looking at it again. It *made* Wes her daddy, somehow: a little girl like Ashley had a vagina, and a daddy like Wes had a hard cock to put there, whenever he wanted—and to put even in the places where it didn't really belong, but where a daddy still likes to have his cock, to make himself feel good.

"Lie back," Wes said gently but with an air of command that Ashley thought she could never disobey now. "Raise your legs and spread your knees wide for me. Hold them open with your hands so that I can see everything I want to see."

Ashley felt her brow furrow. *Everything my daddy wants to see.*

"Do I have to, daddy?" she asked softly.

Wes' voice turned a little stern. "Yes, of course you have to, honey. Remember your promise. If you don't show me your pussy and your bottom right now, I'll need to spank you again."

A thrill of arousal traveled all the way through Ashley's body at this news. She hadn't known, as she spoke the words, why she had asked whether she could get out of exposing herself so shamefully to him; now she did. She didn't want another spanking, really—not *right* now, anyway, because her bottom still felt warm and a little sore from the last one. She *did* want—*need*—to know that Wes wouldn't hesitate to teach her another lesson like the first, if she disobeyed him.

"Please don't spank me, daddy!" she exclaimed, feeling

her whole heart taken over by this powerful idea, that she *did* need the discipline only her Navy SEAL daddy could give her. "Please!"

"Then get those legs up, honey. Right now. Daddy wants to see your little pussy, so I can get it ready for fucking."

"Wh-what does that mean?" Even though she no longer had any doubts at all about whether she wanted to have this kind of relationship—a kind she had never even imagined before today—she kept finding that Wes had an endless ability to say things that kept Ashley nearly on the edge of panic, so arousing and shameful and dominant did they sound.

"Ready for fucking?" he said, with a crooked, wolfish smile that almost took her breath away. "It means that when I put my cock in there, I can pop your cherry nice and quick, and make my little girl feel better between her legs before you even know it hurts. I'm going to get you so wet and ready for daddy's cock that you beg me to put it in there even though you're still my sweet little virgin girl." As he spoke, he advanced two slow steps toward where she lay in the middle of the bed, and now she realized that the height of the bed put her pussy just on a level with the hard length of his manhood, which he held now in his right hand again, stroking it—the sight that had made her feel so faint in the tub, when he had first taken off his jeans and Ashley had seen a man's hard penis for the first time.

"Oh, daddy," she whispered, and she did start to raise her legs. Wes looked into her eyes and smiled, then he reached out with his hands and took her thighs in them. Ashley gasped as he pulled her effortlessly down the bed toward him. Then, as she moaned in mingled shame and arousal, he spread her open himself, looking no longer into her face but straight down at her private parts, which she herself couldn't see, crane her neck as she might.

"So pretty," he murmured. He let go of her knees, but then he took her own hands in his and moved them onto the backs of her thighs. "Keep them open for me, honey,"

he said, returning his eyes to her face for a moment. "Daddy's in charge of your pussy and your bottom now."

"Yes, sir," she said, reverting to the other way to talk about the man who had awakened in her a need to submit to loving masculine authority that she had never thought she could feel.

He looked down again, and Ashley followed his gaze. Then she drew a sharp breath, for Wes had laid his cock on top of the furrow of her pussy, and she thought he would just thrust it in, despite what he had said.

But then Ashley moaned, because her daddy had started to rub her clit with the head of his cock, and it felt wonderful. She closed her eyes and let her head drop to the mattress behind her, just *feeling* the arousal and thinking about how big and strong her daddy was. How he would enter her with his cock and move it in and out, whether she liked it or not.

She liked it so much, though. So much.

"See, honey?" her daddy asked softly.

"Yes, daddy," she whispered, raising her head and feeling her brow furrow deeply as she saw him, naked and looking down at the place where he had put just the tip of his penis inside her, still moving it gently up and down. With three fingertips of his left hand, now, he started to make circles on her clit, and that made her cry out and bite her lip. "Please, daddy!"

"You're very wet, aren't you, young lady?"

"Yes, daddy!"

"Do you want your daddy to fuck you now?"

"Yes, daddy! Please, daddy!" Ashley felt completely delirious. The strangest thing was that it still felt to her like he was in control, like he was making her, despite the way that he had so thoroughly prepared her to lose her virginity to his thrusting cock. It was like having your cake and eating it, too; she could feel both cared for and submissive. She could fall in love with that feeling, she realized.

I could fall in love with my daddy.

She closed her eyes, and suddenly the hard thing inside came up against the place where it hurt. She gave a little cry and bit her lip again.

"Can you be brave, honey?" Wes said.

Ashley nodded, opening her eyes to look into his just for a second; her daddy gazed straight back at her with an expression of affection so strong that it made her smile despite the discomfort down below. He looked down again, though, at the place where his cock had come inside Ashley's pussy. He put his left hand on her thigh, opening her even further despite Ashley having already spread her legs as wide as she thought she could spread them. With his right hand he rubbed her clit, three fingertips round and round until she moaned again.

She felt the muscles in his body tense, and then he pushed very hard and there was a burning flash of pain down there, so intense that for a moment Ashley felt her body trying to escape up the bed, all of its own accord. But her daddy held her in place with that left hand, and he stayed motionless with his cock inside her.

He looked into her eyes again, still rubbing her clit. "That feels so good, honey. It feels wonderful to be inside your little pussy. A daddy loves to have big-girl time inside a tight young vagina like this one."

Ashley was still breathing hard from the pain, which had quickly dulled though her pussy still burned, and it felt so strange to be open around her daddy's hard penis.

"Thank you, daddy," she whispered, letting her mind get caught up into Wes' dirty talk as his fingers made the pain more ambiguous, more a mixture of different, extreme kinds of pleasure. "I'm glad my pussy feels nice."

"So nice, Ashley. Keep holding those knees open, okay? Daddy is going to fuck you now."

She moaned as the thrusting began, every one a powerful surge deep inside her. An animal side of Wes seemed to take him over, as if the pleasure Ashley's body provided had overcome his care and even his thought for her. He kept

rubbing her clit, but though the discomfort became less and the tautness of the muscles in her spread legs seemed to send waves of pleasure through her body, she felt like her enjoyment only mattered because her daddy wanted to be sure he could fuck her whenever he wanted; if his little Ashley didn't mind it so much, he wouldn't have to punish her when she refused to spread her legs for her daddy to put his penis inside her young vagina. She could hardly begin to understand why it felt *good* to know that Wes cared only for his own pleasure—that he hadn't said anything about the risk of getting Ashley pregnant and, now, as he pounded his hips into her bottom, his cock moving swiftly in and out, he fixed his eyes downward to see how a pussy looked with a man's hard length claiming it.

If she got pregnant, she had no doubt Wes would take care of her. It would be a kind of left turn in her life—but a much better left turn than the one she had made into the police car. She looked into his stern face, still not sure why she should love to be only the little thing he used to make his cock feel good, and her heart filled with affection as he looked up from the place where he took his pleasure and into her eyes and smiled, slowing his rhythm.

"So good, honey. Daddy loves fucking his little girl. Does your pussy feel better now?"

"Yes, daddy." It did, but it still also hurt. Ashley tried to smile bravely.

"Daddy's going to turn you over now." Ashley felt her eyes go wide. He had said she would have to have his cock in her bottom... surely he wouldn't do that now, make her take him that way now.

"Don't worry, honey," he said, clearly seeing the panic in her eyes. "I won't fuck your bottom today. But I want to teach you a way to fuck that daddies really like, and I'm going to come inside your pussy that way."

"Okay, daddy," Ashley said hesitantly. Then she added in a whisper, "If we have a baby..."

"Would you like to have a baby, honey?" her daddy

asked, smiling.

Ashley blushed and nodded.

"Well, then," he said gently. "Daddy will finish in your little vagina as often as he likes. He'll finish in your mouth and your bottom, too, sometimes, but he's got enough seed to go around. From now on, you're going to have sex every day. Daddy won't be able to keep from having you with his cock."

The words were so shameful, but Ashley felt her pussy flutter around her daddy's cock as she heard them.

"Okay, daddy," she breathed.

CHAPTER TEN

Wes pulled out and turned her over. His dominant blood had risen so high he couldn't resist—nor did he have any desire to deny himself this pleasure, since Ashley clearly loved it as much as he did. He put two pillows under her hips, spread her knees, and entered her from behind the way he loved to do, his hands on her hips and his cock driving in with abandon. Her little body under his big one, the feeling of her pert bottom against his hips giving him a delicious anticipation of the delight he would have when he fucked her there, her cries of mingled discomfort and pleasure into the mattress: they all combined in his mind and his senses to drive him very quickly to the point of orgasm.

Yes, he would come in her pussy, and maybe he would make a baby inside his sweet little eighteen-year-old girl. The thought of her with a big belly, of taking care of her, seemed to him almost unbearably sexy. At it, he gave a cry and held himself in deep, loving the little sob Ashley made at the feeling of his oncoming orgasm. His cock pulsed and he grunted with the spasming of his muscles, letting the pleasure flow through and just enjoying the feeling of having deflowered the pretty girl he had taken in hand,

spanked, washed, and caressed.

All mine. Maybe the universe had decided to pay him back a little.

He took her into the shower again, just to help her wash up and to hold her as the warm water ran down their bodies, and then he dried her off gently. He put the covers back on the bed and snuggled her up inside them. Early spring in the mountains wasn't too warm for the comforter, so they could hold each other close with the softness all around, still enjoying their nakedness but sated, erotically speaking.

Ashley, of course, wanted to play with her daddy's cock, but when Wes said with a chuckle, "Careful, honey, or you'll have to take it inside your pussy again," her eyes opened wide in alarm and she pulled her naughty hand back.

"I need to tell you about why I left the military," Wes said then. He wasn't certain why he felt it was so important to tell Ashley this story now. Maybe their growing intimacy just demanded that he share the big thing he hadn't told her yet, or maybe he wanted her to understand how much ageplay meant to him. Either way, he knew that taking care of his little girl required honesty in this matter.

They lay on their sides, and Ashley lifted her chin a little to look into his face, wearing a puzzled expression. "Okay, daddy," she said, though she clearly felt some mystification about why he wanted to talk about it now.

"Overseas, I met a girl…" Ashley frowned, but Wes quickly went on, "I didn't have a relationship with her, really—nothing romantic."

"Then what?" She didn't have any accusation in her voice, just curiosity as to what it had to do with her.

"She… well, she was from a very different culture—a whole different world, really—but I could tell she was a little, like you."

"Like me? But you didn't… you know…" Another frown.

"No. See, the thing is, honey, that playing daddy and little girl doesn't have to be about sex at all. It can just be

about candy and coloring."

Ashley giggled. "And spankings?"

"Well, usually spankings, too. That tends to be an important part." Wes felt his heart getting lighter as he shared the story with her. "But I didn't even spank Marmara—that was her name. I just talked about it a couple of times. I guess it was flirting, but we both knew it wasn't anything more than play."

"So... what happened? How did that make you leave the navy?"

Wes felt his smile disappear, and saw the more serious expression reflected in Ashley's face.

"The local warlord... there's no nice way to say it... he gave her to his cousin."

"What?" Ashley's brow clouded over. "Like..."

"He said his cousin could take her as his wife, but it's not like marriage here... I mean..."

Ashley nodded, taking her upper lip between her teeth. "She was going to be raped."

Wes nodded himself. "I... well, Marmara came to me, crying, and I tried to get the warlord to take it back. It wasn't what I was supposed to be doing, but I just couldn't let it happen."

"Oh, God," Ashley said. "Oh, poor daddy. What did you do?"

Wes took a deep breath. "I killed him. He attacked me, and I... I was just so angry. I shot him. And I got court-martialed for it."

"Oh, daddy." She buried her face in his chest. "I'm so sorry."

"I'm sorry, too. I shouldn't have done it. I don't know if I could have saved Marmara otherwise, but I should have tried."

Ashley looked up again. "You saved her?"

Wes let a little smile creep back onto his face as he nodded. "An aid organization took her in as a refugee. I don't know where she is now, and I think it's probably

better that way, but they keep me posted and tell me she's doing fine."

Ashley gave a tentative little smile herself. "I hope she found a daddy of her own."

Wes couldn't help grinning at that. "Because she can't have yours?"

Ashley shook her head. "Nope." Then her face crumpled a little. "Oh, that poor girl. I mean, in Tall Oaks the warden… he was going to…" He felt her tears against his chest.

"Shh," Wes said, holding her closer. "Daddy's here."

• • • • • • •

They spent the whole afternoon in bed, and then Wes made dinner for them.

"Tomorrow," he said before he left the bedroom, "you'll start your chores. I bet you don't know how to cook, but you're going to learn. You'll do that, and you'll clean and you'll do the laundry."

Ashley pouted a little at this news.

"You're going to do a woman's traditional work, honey. That's the way I want it, and it will help you learn respect and obedience. If you don't do your chores, you'll have another trip across my knee. And you'd better wipe that pout off your face, too, or you're going to have one even sooner."

Ashley swallowed hard. "Yes, sir."

"Good girl. You may play outside if you'd like, but don't go up to the road, please. Dinner will be ready in an hour, and then we'll go to bed right afterward so I can fuck you again before you get some good shut-eye."

He loved the way this embarrassing news stained Ashley's cheeks pink.

"But, daddy, I'm so sore down there," she protested.

"I know, honey. Daddy will be as gentle as he can be, but he needs to have his cock in his little girl's pussy again

today. I'll fuck you there one more time before we shave you between your legs tomorrow. I want my Ashley to have a bare pussy, but your fur down there is very cute, too, and I want to say goodbye to it properly."

"Do I really have to be shaved? It's so embarrassing, daddy!"

"Of course it's embarrassing, honey." Wes looked into Ashley's eyes to make sure she was taking this as part of their ageplay life and not as an arbitrary humiliation he had decided to inflict. He thought he could tell that although she undoubtedly had never considered shaving her pussy, the idea that her daddy wanted her bare down there aroused her with its hint of degradation through innocence restored. "That's part of why I'm going to do it."

She pouted again, more theatrically this time. "I don't understand."

"I think you do understand, but not in a way you can really talk about. I think you do want your privates to be nice and tidy for your daddy, because your daddy wants them that way. I think it makes you feel closer to me." He spoke slowly and gently, so that he could gauge the effect of his words and so that he could be sure Ashley would absorb them fully. Then he smiled, still looking into her eyes and waiting to see if she would try to deny it.

Ashley didn't make the attempt: her nose wrinkled and her brow furrowed, and Wes could tell that he had gotten her warm between her legs, because she fidgeted a little where she sat on the edge of the bed while he stood in front of her.

"But that's something that may take a while for you to be able to confess," he went on. "The more important reason I'm going to shave your pussy is that I don't want you be able to hide your pussy when I take down your panties. When I tell you take your clothes off, I want to see that cute little private part peeking out at me."

Her nose wrinkled even more, and she chewed her lips. "Oh," she whispered.

"Are you wet, honey?" he asked with a half-smile.

She looked down at her hands in her naked lap. Her breasts, pushed forward a little by the way she held her arms, seemed to have slightly stiffer peaks than they had a few moments before. "Yes, daddy."

"Do you think you want daddy's cock inside you again today, even though you're sore?"

Now, though she still looked down at her clasped hands, Wes saw her mouth twist to the side as if she tried to hide and suppress a smile. "Yes, daddy."

"Well, be a good girl for daddy and daddy will fuck you after dinner just like he promised."

She looked up at him, her eyes once again wide at the dirtiness Wes could mix in with the care and the comfort. "I'll try, daddy," she said.

• • • • • • •

After dinner, he taught Ashley how to do the dishes without a dishwasher. She didn't sass him, but Wes could tell that she would find it difficult to get used to having actual chores to do around the house.

"You'll do the dishes by yourself from now on," he said. "As I've said, you're going to live a traditional life here with me."

Ashley didn't respond to that. She had seemed to enjoy the burgers and salad he had made, and he had thought once or twice she almost spoke up to say that she didn't think she could cook. But he had cut that off by telling her that she would make spaghetti with tomato sauce and a salad for their next dinner. That news seemed to quiet the almost bratty expression on her face.

When they had finished the dishes, he said. "Okay, honey, go into the bedroom and take your clothes off. Bend over the bed and put your hand between your legs and play with your little pussy until daddy gets there. Daddy's going to train your bottom for a little while before he fucks your

pussy."

"T-train?" Ashley stammered, turning to him.

"It will make it easier when the time comes for you to take daddy's cock in there. I'll start with my fingers, and then I'll put a little plug in your cute anus to teach you how to open and get you used to having something big back there."

A nose wrinkle. "I'm scared, daddy," she said, though Wes felt sure he could detect the same arousal in her eyes that all his wicked suggestions seemed to provoke. "Won't it hurt?"

"It'll be a little uncomfortable at first, honey—especially when I fuck you there. But anal sex is very important to me, and so you're going to have it regularly. I'll do my best to get you ready, and that's what your little lesson tonight is all about. Don't think you can get out of it, though. When your daddy wants to fuck your bottom, he's going to fuck your bottom."

"But why?" she pleaded, her tone getting a little whiny.

"Because I said so, honey. I've taken you in hand, and that means all of you. Your little bottom is a place I'm going to enjoy having my cock, and so you'll have regular anal sex whether you're reluctant about it or not. Now quit talking back and get going. Everything off and bent over the bed, with your hand on your pussy. If you get yourself nice and wet, you'll enjoy your anal training more."

CHAPTER ELEVEN

Ashley dragged her feet as she went from the kitchen toward the bedroom. To her surprise, though, she realized suddenly that she didn't drag them because of her actual anxiety about the lewd things Wes had informed her he would now do to her. She dragged them instead because she wanted Wes to notice her slow, shuffling step, and to tell her that if she dawdled he would punish her. Spank her or switch her or... put something much too big in her bottom.

"Young lady, did you hear me? Get going, or I'm going to spank that little bottom before I plug it." His deep, rumbly voice seemed to send shivers down her spine almost any time she heard him utter a word, but most of all when he told her to do something and he didn't say *please*. And the shivers became almost unbearable when Wes made it clear how ready he was to apply his firm hand to her bare rear end.

"Yes, daddy," she said, turning her head back over her shoulder to look at him, standing in his kitchen like—well, like one of the oak trees she had played among before dinner. She almost gave him the little pout she had tried a few minutes before, but now she really did fear that he would spank her for that. In her eyes now she tried to

communicate that she had never imagined she might have to have her bottom trained, have to have her pussy shaved, have to bend over and play with herself so that her vagina would be ready for a man's hard penis. With her hastening feet, at the same time, she tried to tell him that although she thought she could never admit it in so many words, when she had gone out to play she had started to understand just how much she needed to feel little, and taken in hand by a man who knew how to set boundaries for a girl like Ashley.

I'm going out to play, she had thought, as she left the cabin and emerged into the fresh-smelling woods where the last of the snow crunched under her feet, wearing one of Wes' hoodies and a pair of his boots stuffed with extra socks. It seemed hard to believe that just the day before the snow had seemed so awful and nightmarish as she tried to make her way through it to the road.

Ashley couldn't remember even approximately when the last time would have been when she had gone out to play. Had her parents *ever* told her that, or allowed it? She went to the mall, or to the kids' club at the gym. She remembered that. Recess at school was a thing, she supposed, but teachers didn't say, *time to go out to play*. The bell just rang, the kids poured out into the playground, and if you were like Ashley you stood around awkwardly with your friends and talked about boys.

She supposed that in the time before she could really remember, she had been one of the kids who climbed on the play structure and played pretend games about pirates and things. Now, here among these amazing trees, with what must be her new daddy's workshop visible right next to his cabin, she found that she didn't know how to start.

She *wanted* to start playing, though. When Wes had first told her to go outside and play, her conscious mind had scorned the idea even as something deeper seemed to respond to it eagerly. She looked at the workshop again. Would Ashley have to sweep it tomorrow, maybe? Daddy said Ashley had to do chores, like a good girl in an old-

fashioned house. Ashley would have to learn to keep things neat and tidy, just like Ashley's pussy would be neat and tidy for daddy after tomorrow.

She blushed furiously at that thought, and without even intending it she hid behind a tree so that if her daddy were in his workshop he wouldn't be able to see her and tell her to sweep the floor. When she realized what she had done, hiding that way, she giggled, and suddenly she had figured out how to play.

She played pirates in the woods. The pirates were coming up the mountain to get the princess, and the princess knew that if they got her they would do terrible things to her. That thought made her cheeks get hot, too, because as soon as Ashley thought of the idea of terrible things, she thought of what her daddy had done to her already, and how even though when he had turned her over and put his penis inside her from the back like that, she had felt like he should do that to her because he clearly liked to have his little Ashley that way.

Pirates would do that, too, wouldn't they? They would lay Ashley on her tummy so that they could have her… *fuck* her… just as Wes had done, with their big bodies covering her little one so that she would have to confess that she liked it, and that she *wanted* to stay there with the hard penis going back and forth in her young private part. The next pirate would be standing behind, holding his own penis, waiting for his turn inside little Ashley's vagina.

The first one would get up, once he had filled Ashley's womb with pirate seed, but he would warn her gruffly to stay lying there on her tummy on the ground, because five other pirates were waiting their turns. He would make her admit that she didn't want to get up, and make her say that if she tried to get up, they should flog her with their cat o' nine tails. No, filthy, slutty Princess Ashley needed to take all their cocks, and then she needed a very sore backside. Because Princess Ashley was like that: Princess Ashley loved big pirate cocks.

Dodging between the trees, keeping an eye out for pirates, letting this wicked fantasy unfold in her mind, Ashley could hardly believe she had thought she didn't know how to play outside. She even gave herself over to the fantasy so much that she started to speak her lines, just whispering them.

"My daddy is the only man allowed to touch me there!" she said to the pirate captain who boldly thrust his hand between her thighs. "He's going to catch you and your men! Don't hold me down like that! What are you doing? Only my daddy is allowed to put his cock in me!"

She giggled then, as if to prove to herself that as intense and surprising as these fantasies and the cravings they told of were, she enjoyed letting them out—and she enjoyed *playing* them out with her new daddy Wes—very much indeed.

Now, as she took her clothes off once again, she wondered whether the pirate captain would know how to train a bottom properly. Probably not, she reflected. Only a caring daddy would do that, because he knew that a little girl who had to have anal sex needed lessons so that it wouldn't frighten her, and so that when the time came for her daddy to have her bottom he would enjoy himself fully, the way he had a right to enjoy himself there.

Ashley already loved the way her bottom seemed so precious to her daddy, like a special treasure that he would use to make both of them happy. Her daddy punished her on her bare bottom, and he would train her there. When he put his penis in her pussy, he liked to do it with her bottom up and toward him, so that he could hold it and look at it. Someday soon he would even put his penis right up her bottom itself, and after that he would do it all the time, because it was important to him to do that.

She wanted to turn around and see what Wes was doing now—how close he had gotten to coming into his bedroom to have big-girl time with his little Ashley. But the thought of the look she might see on his face, and the stern words

he might say if she dawdled any more in getting ready for his pleasure, made her stay with her back to the door as she took off the sweatshirt and his oversized t-shirt. She pictured him looking at her from the kitchen, seeing her bra strap, enjoying the view he wanted of the girl he had taken in hand, and she blushed yet again.

Was she really scared he might spank her if she turned around? Yes, but… no. Didn't she feel like she wouldn't mind feeling his firm hand on her bottom, teaching her how it would be in his house, from now on? Didn't she feel like he would never actually punish her for something like that, no matter how much he might play at it?

Ashley had no doubt at all that if she failed to do her chores she would end up over Wes' knee for a real punishment that she certainly did fear, no matter how much she now felt like she might actually need his discipline. But though she couldn't define for herself exactly why, Wes had also made it very clear to her, perhaps when he was talking about the girl overseas and what he had done to protect her, that the big-girl time stuff—the *sex* stuff—was play, even if in the course of the play her daddy knew how to turn his little girl on with threats of spanking and—Ashley swallowed hard as she pulled down her jeans and then her panties—other kinds of punishment.

She stepped out of her jeans. Then she noticed that she had just left her clothes lying on Wes' bedroom floor. With a conscious realization that the duties of a traditional young woman involved keeping the rooms of her daddy's house tidy, she picked them up and folded them, careful to keep her naked back to the door and still picturing Wes watching from the kitchen as she went about this tiny chore. She hoped suddenly that her daddy would praise her for tidying up his room, even though she had created the mess.

"Good girl," came his voice behind her, then, as if he had read her mind. He must be right outside his bedroom door. Was he just passing by on his way to some other daddy activity that little girls didn't get to take part in, or had he

taken a stand there to watch Ashley's every obedient—or *dis*obedient—movement? "You can put your clothes on the dresser. Then go ahead and do as daddy told you, please."

She risked a look over her shoulder. Wes stood right there, smiling, with his hands on his hips. His blue eyes seemed to twinkle at her, as if by folding the clothes she had indeed shown herself to be her daddy's good little girl. The thought made her tummy give a flip-flop, as her body responded, without any conscious will of Ashley's own, to the idea that daddies train good girls' bottoms the same way they train naughty girls'. That daddies fuck good girls the same way they fuck naughty ones, because daddies like to fuck, and daddies are in charge.

The dark blue comforter on the bed, which Wes had tidied and made up, maybe after Ashley had gone out to play, looked as soft as Ashley knew it felt, having spent the whole afternoon wrapped up in it with her daddy's warm, naked body against hers. Ashley would have to make the bed tomorrow, wouldn't she? She knew how to do that at least—not that she had had to do it at home in Westchester, but they had made the girls at Tall Oaks make their own beds. Now, though, she would keep house for her daddy, the way a good girl does.

But before that… in the hours here, in Wes' bedroom, she had to bend over that soft comforter, with her back to her daddy. Feeling almost hypnotized, she started to lean forward, her hands in front of her. But the right hand—that had to go somewhere else, didn't it? Her cheeks got hot at the thought.

"Spread your feet, honey," Wes said, "and bend your knees a bit. Daddy wants a nice view of your little pussy when you start to touch yourself."

Still leaning over a little and biting her lip, Ashley obeyed her daddy's wicked command, knowing that as she inched her feet apart he could see more and more of her private places.

"All the way over now. Why don't you put your left

elbow right there on the bed and start rubbing your clit for me. That's it, honey. Arch your back a little now, and push out that bottom, like daddy's going to spank you. Show me you know what you need."

"Yes, daddy," Ashley whispered to the bed, trying to push her bottom out the way Wes liked it, so he would give her what she had coming, what she needed, there. Right there.

CHAPTER TWELVE

Wes had bought his two butt plugs, the big black one and the little pink one, when he was dating Julie, but he had never found the right moment to work them into their play. Especially now, with more experience, he felt completely sure Julie would have blushingly welcomed anal play if he had decided to introduce it into their sex life. He had thought once or twice while he dated Angela of punishing her with the big plug, but the occasion for that hadn't arisen either. Now the prospect of training Ashley Lewis' bottom for his cock seemed like the whole reason he had bought the plugs in the first place.

As Ashley began to play with her furry little pussy, rubbing her clit firmly as Wes had instructed and then running her fingertips up and down the sweet pink lips that already glistened with her wetness, Wes opened his top dresser drawer and took the pink plug and the lube from their place. Ashley had turned her face toward the bed and closed her eyes. Wes could just make out the deep crease in her brow as she began to make little whimpering noises at the pleasure she brought to herself.

"Like this, daddy?" she whispered.

"Yes, honey. Just like that. Daddy likes it when his little

girl feels nice."

"But only when you let me?" Her voice sounded strained, as if the dirty little dialogue had ratcheted her arousal up to a level hard to endure.

Wes took a stand behind her and flipped open the top of the lube. "That's right, honey. Only when daddy says you may feel those big-girl feelings. Daddy is in charge of your pussy and your bottom, and he knows that little girls sometimes have grownup thoughts and desires. That's why I play with those parts of you, and put my penis inside them whenever I want."

"Oh, God," Ashley whispered. "Wes..." Her fingers slowed in the adorable curls between her thighs.

Wes stopped in the midst of applying lube to the little pink plug. "Yes, honey?" he asked in his regular, non-dirty-daddy voice.

"Isn't it wrong?"

"No, honey. If we both have fun, it's not wrong. Things are only wrong when someone gets hurt, as far as I've ever been able to figure out."

"But..." Suddenly, as if she simply couldn't control it, Ashley's fingers started to move again, and she whimpered, "You spank me. That hurts."

Wes smiled, a cloud of concern lifting from his heart. "Well, I guess I mean hurt in a bad way. I think I can see that you know what I mean, you naughty girl."

"Daddy!" The fingers moved even faster up and down and around her clit. Wes felt the temptation to forego the anal training and just fuck that sweet little cunt for the last time before he shaved it. The idea that this sweet, wanton little girl belonged to him—her private, pleasurable places and all the rest of her as well—made him feel like an emperor, or an admiral. "I'm being good for you now, aren't I?"

"Yes, honey. Very good. But also very naughty. So naughty you need a lesson in daddy's pleasure. Stay bent over, but reach both your hands back and hold your bottom

open for me."

"Oh, daddy, no. Please!"

He reached out with his right hand, the plug and lube now in his left, and gave her a sharp spank on her right cheek. Ashley made a surprised little cry.

"See? You're still a naughty girl, aren't you? Spread those cheeks or daddy's going to spank them until you do."

"But, daddy, it's so embarrassing!"

"Of course it is, young lady. Daddy wants to see you show him the most private part of your body. I want to teach you that I'm in charge of that part just as much as I'm in charge of the rest of you." Wes gave her another spank, on her left cheek. Her fingers moved frantically at the top of her pussy and the scent of her arousal came deliciously to his nose. "Now. Spread. These. Cheeks," he said sternly, giving a swat at each word.

"Oh, daddy..." Ashley wailed, but even as she did she had begun to obey, her naughty play-with-herself hand moving around and her upper body coming up off the bed slightly as she reached her left hand around, too, then falling to the comforter. She had her little cheeks in her hands, now, and she gave a whimper as if at the lingering pain from the spanks he had given her there, which had left a lovely light pink glow behind. She pulled the globes apart, the whimper changing into a soft, humiliated sob.

"There we go. Was that so hard, my good girl?"

Ashley had turned her cheek to the comforter. Her eyes were bright with unfallen tears at her little spanking. "No, daddy," she mumbled.

Wes reached out his right hand and laid the lubed tip of his forefinger on the sweet dimple of her anus. It clenched adorably, but he pressed gently there until, with a moan, Ashley let the finger enter just a bit.

"See?" Wes said. "You can do it, honey." He moved the finger in and out a little. "Doesn't that feel nice?"

"Yes, daddy, but... but it's so strange and... wicked!"

"It's not wicked if daddy says it's not, honey. Daddy likes

to train his little Ashley's bottom, so little Ashley has to spread her cheeks for her lesson. Little Ashley will be grateful for her lessons when the time comes for daddy to put something much bigger in here."

"Oh, no..." Ashley murmured, as if to herself.

"It feels strange and wicked because you never thought you would have to learn to please a man completely," Wes continued, now moving the finger steadily in and out, pushing deeper and deeper and making Ashley gasp. "As daddy trains you to open yourself to him, you'll understand that his pleasure comes first, and that by training you for anal sex he's teaching you to obey him completely."

He looked at her face, lying sweetly on the comforter, eyes closed and her lip caught between her teeth. The little whimpers came continuously, with every thrust of his forefinger.

"Shh. It's time to stretch you a little." Wes added his middle finger, and Ashley gave a startled cry. "Push now, honey. You know how to open your little ring. You do it every day on the toilet."

"Oh, daddy!" Her cheek went pink and she seemed to shut her eyes even more firmly. Her bottom clenched against his intrusion, but Wes moved his fingers insistently, to teach her that the filling of her anus would go on just as he liked, whenever he liked. "Oh, I can't!"

"You can, Ashley. I promise." He pulled his fingers out. "It will be a little easier with this." He shifted the pink plug, three inches long with a tapered head and a flared base, almost as thick at its middle as a man's cock, to his right hand.

"With what, daddy?" she said in alarm, her eyes flying open.

He showed her. "Daddy will use this to train his little girl's bottom," he said matter-of-factly.

"No, please..." Ashley said. "It's too big!"

"It's not as big as your daddy's cock, honey, and you're going to have my cock in your bottom-hole before too

long."

She closed her eyes, then opened them. He could see that though the newness of the idea that Wes would enjoy her bottom just as he pleased had created a little fear, she still felt the fascination and even the craving he had seen in her face before.

"Daddy's going to put the plug in now, honey, whether you like it or not. Anal training isn't optional for you. It's an important part of your life here."

He put the narrow tip right at her little ring. She gave a whimpering cry and closed her eyes, squeezing the pert globes in her fingers as if trying to soothe away a smart that hadn't yet come. Then Wes pushed, gently at first but with steadily increasing force, for a few seconds. Ashley tensed against the intrusion, and he stopped pushing.

"Push, honey," he said. "You know you can. Pull those cheeks apart and push."

"But it's so embarrassing, daddy!"

"We've been through this, Ashley. It's supposed to be embarrassing. Little girls who are learning about their needs have to learn who's in charge of their bodies. Now push with your bottom, and let the plug in." As he spoke the last words, he pushed again, and Ashley spread her bottom wider with her hands and opened to the plug with a sob of shame and discomfort that became a whining cry as he filled her anus with the hard rubber. He kept pushing until at last her tiny bottom-hole closed around the narrow part that came before the flared base, so that only that little base remained outside, primly but lasciviously indicating that Ashley Lewis had accepted her daddy's wishes for her young bottom. "There, honey," Wes said softly. "So pretty with your new plug."

"Oh, daddy," Ashley said, again shutting her eyes tightly as her visible cheek turned an even brighter pink. "Oh, daddy, please take it out!" She moved the halves of her backside back and forth lewdly, as if trying to get used to the feeling of having her anus trained for the cock.

"No, honey," Wes said. "You're going to have it in your bottom while daddy fucks you with his penis. A butt plug makes a girl even tighter for a man's cock. Daddy's going to take off his clothes now, and then he's going to have his way inside you. While I get undressed I want you to think about how tomorrow your grownup hair is going to be gone from your little pussy, and how the next time I fuck you you'll be bare between your legs."

He watched her adorable face carefully—the three-quarters of it he could see as she turned it upon the blue comforter—and saw that his words had the effect he wanted: the lip caught between her teeth again and the furrowed brow.

"Neat and tidy," she whispered.

"Exactly, honey," Wes agreed. "Neat and tidy for your daddy, in your panties."

Ashley gave a little gasp at that, as it the mention of underwear had a special power for her. As Wes stripped his shirt off, she opened her eyes again. To his gratification, she widened them as if at the sight of his well-muscled torso.

"But I only have that one pair of panties, daddy."

"We can do something about that the next time I go into town," Wes replied, "but until then you'll wash your panties every day. A good girl always has clean underwear, doesn't she?"

"Yes, daddy."

Wes unbuckled his belt and stripped off his jeans, knowing the contrast of his own lack of underwear would interest his little Ashley and so he was not surprised to hear what she whispered next.

"But daddies don't have to wear underwear, do they? Over their big, hard cocks?"

Wes chuckled. "No, honey. Daddies get to wear exactly what they want. Do you like to see daddy's cock come out of his jeans that way?"

"Oh, yes, daddy." Ashley's blush, which had faded for a moment, returned full force. "I know I've only had it in my

mouth once and my pussy once, but I love your penis so much. It's so funny: I'm still sore, but I want your penis inside me so bad I would do anything… even have a little pink plug in my bottom." She giggled.

He smiled in response. "Okay, honey. Why don't you move your hands down and open your pussy for me now. Show your daddy where you want his penis."

Ashley closed her eyes again, and moved her hands down from her bottom to the tops of her thighs. She gave a little moan as she obeyed, spreading her furry pussy-lips to show the narrow, velvety cavern where Wes would now take his pleasure. She turned her face to the comforter, as if in respect to his mastery, and Wes enjoyed the sight of his good, lustful little girl offering herself for his use, stroking his cock to aid his arousal at the lewd sight.

He stepped forward and put his cockhead there where Ashley showed him the way, and she gave a happy cry. He thrust in hard, and she cried out differently at the fullness of cock and plug together.

"So tight, honey," he murmured, as the pleasure coursed through his veins and he began his driving rhythm. "Such a tight little girl for her daddy's cock."

With each thrust her cries grew louder and more ambiguous, as if she felt too much for her body even to process: pleasure and pain together becoming something else, something overwhelming.

"Put your hands in front of you, Ashley," he said. "Elbows on the bed. Daddy's going to fuck you hard now."

He put his hands on her shoulders and he did fuck her hard, himself overcome by the incredible pleasure of her tight young pussy and the sight of her bottom tensing around the little pink plug. The feeling of her pert cheeks against his hips as he finished each thrust drove him nearly wild, and it wasn't more than a few minutes before he held himself in at full length and shot his seed inside her.

"Thank you, honey," he said, stroking her hip gently. "You made daddy feel very good." He stepped back, pulling

out and making Ashley give a forlorn little wail. "It's your turn, now." He put his hand on the pussy he had fucked, enjoying the way his semen flowed there now, and began to pleasure his little girl.

"Oh, daddy, no," she said. "It's too... too..." Her voice trailed off into a strangled cry, though. "Oh, God. Daddy... oh... God."

"Too what, honey?" Wes asked, chuckling, wiggling the butt plug gently with his left hand as his right made firm circles around Ashley's clit.

But Ashley couldn't answer with anything but the scream of her first orgasm. As her body tensed, Wes kept rubbing and wiggling. His little girl would have at least five orgasms now, if he had anything to say about it.

CHAPTER THIRTEEN

"Ashley," Wes' voice said. "I'll let you sleep in today, but you should have made me breakfast, and tomorrow you'll do that or there will be consequences."

He had already woken her twice, with gentle backrubs and encouragement to get up and start the day's work, but she had remained immovable, really just out of force of habit. Unless there were detention-center guards threatening her, she always slept in.

"Just be sure to do the dishes and the rest of your chores before I come back from the workshop for lunch, alright? I can get lunch for both of us and then we can start the sauce for dinner together before I go back out."

"Okay," Ashley mumbled from the covers. She realized she hadn't said *daddy* only a split second later, and she almost corrected herself. She could feel Wes still standing there, as if waiting to hear her say "Okay, daddy." But she decided not to say it, though she didn't feel entirely sure why. Really, though the soreness she felt down below had a delicious, submissive quality to it, and though her heart still seemed full of gratitude for Wes' having agreed to take her in, Ashley also felt that probably it would be good to restore some balance.

Wes finally left, closing the door behind him. Ashley sat up only a few moments later, wondering why she felt restless now—wondering why she felt like Wes should have tried harder to get her up, when she had just a few moments ago felt a flash of anger at him for telling her she had to rise and shine. She heard the door of the cabin close: daddy going to his workshop. *Wes* going to his workshop, Ashley corrected herself as she padded to the bathroom, feeling her face get hot at the memory of what had happened there the previous day.

At the idea of what he had said he would do today, where that pleasantly sore region down below was concerned.

She found her breakfast—eggs, bacon, and buttered toast—on the table, covered with another plate. Next to it was a note that made Ashley smile.

I can't wait to see my little girl again. Have a wonderful day! Daddy

Once she'd had breakfast, she surveyed the dishes. There weren't many of them, and Wes had put hot water in the frying pan to soak the egg off, but when she put the plates and cups in the sink it just looked like there were too many to wash, so she decided to take her shower and face them when she felt a little cleaner herself.

In the shower, of course, Ashley couldn't help thinking of the way Wes had talked about shaving her between her legs. She washed herself there self-consciously. Did she really feel more open, where a Navy SEAL who called himself her daddy had thrust in and out, had fucked her twice in a manner that seemed in her memory now so commanding and shameful, making her keep her face to the bed as he rode her in pursuit of his own pleasure? Where he had proven that he knew how to force Ashley's own pleasure upon her, until she screamed with it and came over and over, sobbing for it to end even as she felt desperate for more?

And she wasn't allowed to touch herself there without permission, now, was she? Ashley found that at the thought of what Wes had done with his cock and his hands and the little pink plug she had started to move her fingers fretfully among the curls Wes had said he would take away, so that she made little whining sounds in her chest. The warm water just felt so good, and her fingers there, soothing the soreness, so delicious.

Guiltily, though, she pulled her hand away and finished her shower, washing between her bottom-cheeks with only the slightest exploration of whether the plug had changed her at all. She blushed anew when she realized that she could open to her finger now, but when the wicked thought occurred that maybe her daddy would want her to wash herself inside her bottom, now that he planned to enter her there with his penis, she pushed it firmly away, rinsed herself off, and turned the tap to end the shower and force herself to get on with the day.

She realized as she stepped back toward the bedroom, clad in a towel, that she hadn't washed her panties. But Wes had washed them the previous night, right? And she hadn't even worn them very much the day before. He wouldn't notice. She pulled them on, then her jeans and the t-shirt and hoodie from the day before.

On the counter she found another note, a to-do list.

Little Ashley's Chores
Make bed
Dishes
Sweeping (broom in kitchen closet)
Clean bathroom (supplies under sink)
Smile for daddy

There was a little heart after *Smile for daddy*. Ashley did smile, but then she felt foolish. She looked again at the dishes in the sink. Didn't Wes know that she hated doing dishes? That yucky feeling of the dirty water, and the bits of

food in it—even the thought of it made her tummy revolt. How could he make her do something she hated that much? Real people had dishwashers: real people put the plates in, pushed the button, and then they took the shiny dishes out of the machine.

Making the bed didn't present a problem, though. She went to do that, and then she didn't even look at the sink as she went to get the broom. She swept the living room slowly, but she tried to do a good job, and the amount of dust she collected in there and in the bedroom made her feel like she had done a reasonable job.

She even cleaned the toilet, since it already looked pretty clean. She could do her chores, like Wes told her. Like daddy told her. She felt her cheeks get pink, remembering the little heart on the to-do list, and the way she had smiled at it.

She went outside, careful not to go too far up the driveway. From Wes' workshop came the sound of a saw. Somehow in these mountainous woods the high roaring-buzzing sound, echoing through the trees, seemed like the perfect noise to make the whole scene seem perfect: the sun filtering down, the little cabin built with her daddy's own hands, the sound of her daddy making things from the trees that would grow again here on these forested mountains. Just enough chill in the air to make it seem nice to be outside, but even nicer because Ashley had a warm cabin she could go back inside, to wait for her daddy to come in from his workshop.

The saw stopped, and suddenly Ashley remembered she hadn't done the dishes. She stood in the trees, a little uphill from the cabin and the workshop, frozen in place. The workshop door opened. Suddenly the idea that she hated doing the dishes seemed like the stupidest thing in the world, and the thought that her daddy should have known she hated that chore and should have let her do something else instead seemed absurd.

Wes emerged, with safety-goggle marks around his eyes and a little bit of sawdust clinging to his flannel shirt. So big

and so handsome. Ashley's eyes went straight to his powerful hands. *Oh, no.*

She tried to call out, *Daddy, stop. Wait! I'll do the dishes! Just give me a second!* But the words stuck in her throat as Wes walked to the front door of the cabin, not noticing her, and opened it.

Consequences. Ashley's tummy flip-flopped much worse than it had at the thought of the dishes. Much, much worse. How could she have earned another punishment so quickly? She started to run toward the cabin. Maybe if she said she was sorry, and she would do the dishes right now, her daddy wouldn't spank her.

But as she reached the door she heard him calling, "Ashley?" in his stern voice, and her heart fell. She stopped just outside the door, looking at it, feeling her eyes go wide in alarm at the thought of what his face must look like.

She almost ran away, but honestly she felt too scared even for that.

The door opened and Wes stood there, looking at her. A look of concern on his face changed to one of authority.

"You're in big trouble, young lady," he said grimly. "It was fine to leave the house, but you should have left a note, or come to tell me you were going outside."

Ashley felt her brow furrow. "Sorry, daddy." Now she felt close to tears.

"And that's before we get to the dishes. You did a fine job with the other chores, but the sink is still full of the breakfast things. I even put that on your list."

"I know, daddy, but…"

"But what, honey?"

"I hate doing dishes." It sounded so lame to Ashley's own ears that she couldn't keep her eyes raised to his but had to lower them to his big leather work boots.

"Honey, I don't want this to sound too harsh, but I don't care whether you hate this or that chore. You have chores to do, and they're not all that hard. You're going to do them, or you're going to be punished. And if I have to I can keep

punishing you until you understand that. Go into the kitchen and do those dishes right now. Then take off your clothes, get a towel, put it on the bed, and lie on it with your knees up and spread like I showed you yesterday when I popped your cherry. I'm going to shave you before I spank you."

"Oh, daddy, no!" The thought of the shaving had seemed bad enough when it was just a sex thing. Now that Wes had put it in the category of discipline it seemed so much more humiliating. To have her pussy bared that way before her daddy took her over his knee... she wasn't sure she had yet blushed as hotly as she did then, thinking about it.

"And if you think that's all, young lady, you've got another think coming. After your spanking, you'll have a figging."

"A *what?*" Ashley had not the slightest idea what Wes meant, but the word itself seemed to drip with shame.

"A ginger plug up your bottom, to keep in for an hour. You'll help me start the sauce that way, naked except for your apron."

The idea made Ashley feel faint. "Wh-why *ginger?*" she whispered, meeting his eyes again in her alarm. She had no experience cooking: ginger was something you put in ginger ale or, she guessed, ginger snaps. It had a *sharp* taste, right?

Wes looked back grimly, his eyes narrowing a little. "You'll see, honey. It won't feel as nice as the little pink plug last night."

"What does that mean?" Ashley said, but Wes didn't answer. Her heart started to race. "Daddy? What does that mean?"

As if at the fright in her voice and the way she had called him *daddy*, Wes' face seemed to get softer and kinder. "It means that ginger burns a bit, honey. Not so as to harm you, or even hurt you very much, but to make you pretty uncomfortable in that cute little anus of yours. And of course to embarrass you when you think about what you did

wrong and how I'm looking at a well-disciplined backside with a ginger plug sticking out, because I put it there to teach you your lesson."

Ashley's face got even hotter, and her eyes fell again. Almost unconsciously, she put her right hand back to the seat of her jeans as if to ward off the horrid thing. How could she bear it? And yet Wes had made her duties very clear, and also made it clear that she would be punished if she didn't do them. Ashley had earned the consequences.

"Get going, Ashley," Wes said sternly. "Neither of us is going to have lunch until you've had your spanking and your figging, and then we've got the sauce to start after that. I'll go back to my workshop for fifteen minutes. When I get back, I want you naked and ready for shaving."

CHAPTER FOURTEEN

Wes found Ashley just the way he wanted her, after he had checked to make sure she'd done the dishes. He brought the basin, filled with hot water, and several washcloths, along with the scissors he used to trim his own hair, a new disposable razor, and some soap and lotion for afterward. He was glad to see the pretty sight of a furry little pussy between raised and spread thighs, well presented to his gaze as he entered the room.

"I'm sorry, daddy," Ashley said as he approached, before he could even see her face. "I did the dishes."

"I saw, honey. Thank you." He stood over her and looked down into her eyes.

She returned his gaze with a troubled brow. "Maybe... maybe you could just shave me? And then, you know, you could..." Her cheeks turned pink as she looked at him between her knees, over the sweet pussy Wes loved to see so exposed and ready for his attention.

"Fuck my little girl?" Wes asked, smiling.

Ashley bit her lip. "Or I could, you know, suck your penis? To show I'm sorry?"

He kept his smile, but shook his head. "You can't get out of a punishment by giving your daddy pleasure, honey.

And I have to make it clear to you that I'll follow through when I discipline you. After I shave you, I'm going to spank you and fig you. You're not getting out of it."

Her eyes got bright with tears. She let go of her knees and her legs started to drop. "Oh, daddy! I promise to be good!"

"Get those knees up and hold them wide, Ashley," Wes said sternly. "Don't make this worse for yourself."

She obeyed, but she wailed at the same time, "But daddy…"

"Hush, honey. We both know you need this. Lie back and let daddy get you nice and smooth. If you take your punishment well today, daddy will kiss his little girl's pussy tonight and make her feel very good, as a reward."

Ashley gave a little whimper at that, as if at the wicked thought of her daddy's mouth on her bare privates, and didn't finish what she had been going to say—if indeed she had had anything to say at all.

Wes pulled the wooden chair from the corner of his bedroom up to the bed. He put the basin on the floor as he sat.

"I'm going to trim your pussy hair nice and short, then I'm going to use some hot washcloths to make you nice and soft for the razor." He didn't wait for a reply, which in fact didn't come except in the form of some gasping breaths from Ashley, but went to work grasping tufts of the curly reddish brown hair between her thighs and neatly trimming it off, until every bit of it longer than a millimeter lay in a cute little heap on the towel.

As he trimmed her pussy fleece with the scissors, Ashley giggled a little as it got ticklish, but she held herself obediently open. Wes felt some satisfaction as he saw that a little bit of slippery moisture seemed to have developed between the tender coral lips that peeped out just a bit from the bigger, paler ones, but he said nothing about it.

"What do I look like, daddy?" Ashley whispered.

"You look cute as a button, honey," Wes said. "Already

very neat and tidy. It would be very scratchy, though, if I didn't shave you."

She giggled, the punishment forgotten for a moment. "Would it be scratchy for you when you put your penis inside me?"

Wes felt himself crook a smile at the dirty talk. "Yes, but it would be even scratchier for you inside your panties."

"Oh," Ashley said with a little shudder. Then, as Wes put the hot washcloths in place, over her mons and down all the way to her little anus where a few naughty hairs lingered, she sighed. "Daddy, I didn't wash my panties. I'm sorry."

Wes chuckled. "That's alright, honey. Thanks for telling me. You're a good girl to confess that. You won't need them again today, and you can wash them tonight after sex. They'll be dry in the morning."

A little shiver seemed to go through her at the words *after sex*, which was just the effect Wes had meant to achieve.

"After sex?" she said softly.

"Yes, honey. Daddy will have sex with you every night from now on. You can plan to wash your panties after that, each night. Not before, because daddies like to take down their little girls' panties themselves, if they've been allowed panties that day."

Another little sigh, and a wriggle to go along with it, as if the washcloths were having a rather complicated effect in the region to be shaved. "Yes, daddy," Ashley said a little dreamily.

Wes took the washcloths away then and started to lather her between her legs. "This may tickle a little, honey," he said rather wickedly.

"Oh, daddy," Ashley moaned, squirming under his fingers. "Tickle?"

"Yes, tickle," he replied in a firm voice as he applied the lather to the area right around her adorable pink clit.

"Yes, daddy!" Ashley cried, bucking against his hand.

"Are you helping with the lather, honey?" he said as he moved his soapy fingers further down, to find her wetness.

"Yes, daddy!"

"Good girl," he pronounced, and got the razor. "Keep these legs nice and wide for daddy. We'll have the hair gone in no time."

Oh, he loved to see her little pussy clench as he delicately swept the razor down and around, and he loved the scent of helpless arousal as he rubbed gently under the pretext of checking how smooth he had gotten her. The folds of her young privates glistened as he bared them, and it was all Wes could do not to taste them immediately.

Instead, he said when he had trimmed the final embarrassing stubble from around her bottom hole, "Time for lotion, honey. When I put it on, you'll probably have some big-girl feelings, and that's okay. But I want you to remember that you're being punished. Daddy's going to make you show him how much you need his penis, but you aren't allowed to come. Do you understand?"

"I think so, daddy," Ashley said with trepidation in her voice.

Wes rubbed the lotion in thoroughly, while Ashley cried out with forced, shameful pleasure. "Please, daddy... Daddy, please..." she begged, almost as if he were already spanking her. She writhed on the towel, her face a bright red and her eyes closed, as if his admonition that she must not let herself orgasm had made this demonstration of her erotic craving for her daddy's penis a terrible ordeal.

Finally, Wes satisfied himself that he had moisturized the whole precious place he had shaved. He looked at the pussy and the anus where he had decreed that he would find his release at least once a day from henceforward, feeling like he wouldn't mind forgetting about Ashley's punishment and just fucking her in her sweet eighteen-year-old pussy and then in her cute eighteen-year-old backside. But he had taken her in hand, and though he had forgiven her instantly about the dishes, her not having done them and having gone outside instead demonstrated very clearly that she needed a stern lesson.

"Stay like that while daddy cleans up, honey," he said, picking up the basin. "I'll be back to spank you in a few moments."

"Oh, daddy," Ashley whined, but in the pleasured state Wes had put her in, it sounded less distressed than it might have been.

When he returned, bringing the ginger he had cut in a paper towel, and had sat in the chair, once again contemplating the beautiful sight of the newly bare privates of his little girl, he said, "Stand up, Ashley, and put your hands on your head."

He spread his thighs so that she could stand between them, and laid the paper towel with the ginger inside on the bed. The contrast of his jeans and shirt with her nakedness seemed to have its proper effect, and Ashley couldn't meet his eyes as she stood there, gazing at her perfect breasts and the tidy cleft of her pussy.

"Look at me, young lady," he said, and she did, with wide eyes. "You've said you're sorry, and I appreciate that. But we both know the reason you apologized, and the reason you'll do the dishes from now on, is that you know that you live in a house where traditional discipline is maintained. Isn't that right?"

"Yes, daddy." Her voice sounded frightened, just as he wanted her to be.

"You'll call me *sir* when I'm punishing you," Wes said sternly.

"Yes, sir," Ashley whispered, her eyes going even wider.

"Your bare bottom is about to feel the consequences of your actions, and if I can I want to be sure that as I spank you you're reaping the benefit of this lesson. Why are you about to be spanked over daddy's knee, Ashley?"

He reached out to take her hands in his, and gave them a gentle squeeze. Ashley trembled. She looked down at their hands and then back up at Wes.

"Because I didn't respect you, sir," she said with a little sob. "You asked me to do something, and I didn't do it. And

I didn't respect you when I went outside without leaving a note."

Wes didn't waste any time, but released her hands, took her hips in his grasp, and turned her, then upended her over his left thigh. Ashley gasped, and then cried out at the sudden beginning of her punishment, so much more abrupt than he had treated her the day before.

Then he began, again without further delay, to spank her very hard—so hard that she started to scream and struggle within a few seconds. Wes held her tightly with his left arm and put his right leg firmly across her thighs and kept spanking her, going from cheek to cheek and raising his arm high to bring his big hand down with the force needed to make Ashley sorry she had neglected her duty.

He knew that he had driven the arousal from her body with the first few blows, and he closed his ears to his little girl's heartrending cries as he disciplined her so sternly. He kept spanking hard, until her whole backside had turned crimson under his firm hand and she lay limp over his knee, sobbing. Then he reached for the paper towel, unfolded it, and took the ginger, a little plug three inches long, in his right hand.

"Wh-what...?" Ashley sobbed as he used his left hand to open her bottom.

Wes didn't answer, but put the narrow tip of the ginger to the little flower of her anus.

"Oh, no... oh, daddy, please..."

He pushed the ginger in a bit.

"N-not... not yet, daddy... oh, God, please, daddy," Ashley wailed. "Oh, daddy, it burns! Oh, please!"

"It does burn, honey. It's supposed to burn." He pushed further, and satisfied himself that the little plug had seated itself fully inside her. "You will keep it in your anus for an hour. If it falls out, you will have a bigger one, and the hour will begin again."

"No, daddy... please, don't..."

"Hush, Ashley. You've been doing so well. Go get the

apron from the kitchen closet and put it on. We'll start the sauce now."

He opened his legs and helped her stand up. Ashley turned to go, her face streaked with tears and her eyes downcast, but Wes stopped her and enfolded her in his arms. "Are you learning your lesson?" he asked softly, right into his little girl's ear.

"Yes, daddy," she sniffled. "But it hurts so much! My bottom feels like it's on fire! And the ginger… it's just so… I'm sorry I didn't do the dishes."

Wes put his hand down to her bottom to fondle the pert cheeks, now so very warm from their severe punishment. Ashley gave a little sigh and snuggled into him. But Wes couldn't resist giving the ginger a little push that made her jump and drove her even closer to him.

"You'll be sore for a while," he said, "as you should be."
"Yes, sir," Ashley said.

CHAPTER FIFTEEN

Ashley's daddy put his penis in her bottom for the first time that night. After he let her take the ginger out—she had had to eat lunch standing up, of course, still wearing only the apron, and then he made her take the awful, burning little plug out in front of him, bending over to show him just what her bottom looked like with a piece of *root* inside, which made Ashley's face glow as hot as the sun— he told her that she could play for the rest of the afternoon until the time came to finish dinner, and that she would have the reward he had promised that night.

She wasn't to wear anything but the apron for the rest of the day, though, to remind her that she lived in a traditional house, now, where girls did their chores and wore their aprons. And she wasn't to sit on the furniture, because the furniture was for responsible grownups. She could play games on the living room floor she had made so nice and clean: Wes showed her a fairly impressive shelf of card games and board games, for a man who lived alone, most of which could be played solo, alongside books of crossword puzzles and Sudoku.

As she played a dice game where you tried to get different combinations of the numbers on the dice, she

shifted around uncomfortably, trying to find a posture that didn't feel terribly sore. Really, the lingering effects of the hard spanking her daddy had given her weren't nearly as distracting as the heat that remained from the ginger in the anus Wes had started to train with the little pink plug the previous night.

The game didn't require a great deal of concentration, but she still found her hand letting go of the dice cup and making its way behind her, to touch her punished bottom where the apron left it bare and of course so visible to her daddy, whenever he decided to come back from his workshop and have a look at his little girl's bottom—something, Ashley thought with a blush, he obviously liked to do very much. She also found herself nearly unconsciously thanking heaven that he had put her in the apron so that she didn't have easy access to the pussy he had shaved, because after he had spanked her so hard that the terrible arousal of the lotion had gone completely away, that arousal had come back even more achingly into her privates. Together with the ginger the remaining heat from the spanking, the pleasant irritation of her newly bare vagina, and even the very idea that her daddy had bared her there for his pleasure put her in grave danger, she thought, of playing with herself when she heard the whine of the saw that meant her daddy was busy and would never catch her.

But though Ashley did, once or twice, put her middle finger right up against her bottom's little dimple, and though once she couldn't resist kneeling up and bending over the couch so that she could just feel what her privates were like with no curly hair down there, she didn't do anything more than that. She felt proud to be able to answer honestly when Wes, having come back to find that she had finished dinner, still of course in only the apron, asked with narrowed eyes whether she had done anything naughty.

"No, daddy."

"You didn't touch yourself? That can be hard for some little girls, after a spanking."

"No, daddy. But…"

Wes' brow creased slightly, as if he were sure she was about to confess something for which he would have to discipline her.

"But what, honey?"

Ashley's voice fell to a whisper, and her eyes darted from one of his deep blue irises to the other nervously. "But my bottom…"

She hadn't even been sure what she wanted to say, and now she lost her courage and looked down at the buttons on his green plaid shirt.

Did he guess what she meant? "Your bottom will get what's really coming to it tonight, Ashley. I've decided. Tonight's the night."

She looked up again, into his eyes, with alarm but also with the feeling that her daddy had read her mind. Wes nodded.

"After I fuck your pussy, I'm going to fuck your bottom, so you need to make your mind up to please me even though it's uncomfortable. After you're a good girl for your first anal, you'll have that reward we talked about."

"Yes, daddy," Ashley whispered. The one thing she couldn't seem to figure out—that she realized she didn't even want to figure out, for fear of dispelling its magic—was why it felt so wonderful that she hadn't had to admit to Wes that the ginger and the shaving had suddenly made her think, all the time she played the dice game and did crosswords, that she'd like to see what it felt like when a little girl had to let her daddy put his penis in her bottom, and had to let him move it in and out until the seed spurted out there, inside her young anus where a daddy could fuck as much as he wanted and not make a baby.

Her daddy had let her keep the shameful words unsaid; he had allowed her to preserve the idea that the choice lay all with him, the man who had taken her in hand and now used her tender body for his pleasure.

So after dinner, when to her surprise he helped her do

the dishes—maybe because he wanted to see as much of her in nothing but the apron as he could, since he didn't seem to be able to keep from fondling her bottom as she stood at the sink, trying to concentrate on getting the plates clean—she could show a little reluctance when her daddy said, "It's time, honey. Into the bedroom, now."

"But, daddy... please, not my bottom? Not yet?"

"Ashley, what did I tell you? I've decided. Lie on your tummy and put a pillow under your hips. Knees spread nice and wide. Leave the apron on. Daddy is very hard for you. I'll try to be gentle, but it's time for sex, and I don't want to have to punish you again to teach you that I'm in charge."

Ashley felt herself getting unbearably warm down there, under the apron. Her breath came in little pants as she dried the final dish, looking over her shoulder at Wes and seeing the hunger in his eyes. He stood a little behind her, his arms folded over his chest, looking back at her with an expression that said very clearly that he wouldn't hesitate to spank her again if he needed to, before he enjoyed her with his penis. She felt her brow furrow as the reluctance took hold a bit more, much as she knew deep inside that Wes knew exactly what she needed.

Wes unfolded his arms and put his hand down, took her whole bottom in his palm. "This belongs to me, Ashley," he said solemnly. "I decide what to do with it."

"Oh, God," Ashley whispered, feeling the wetness seem almost to gush between her thighs.

"Because you're dawdling, honey, and keeping me waiting, you're going to need to kneel down and suck daddy's cock right now, just to take the edge off."

"But..."

He took his hand from her bottom and started to unbuckle his belt. "Kneel down, Ashley. This instant."

She did. She obeyed him as if her body had a will of its own. He had his jeans down now, and his cock stood up stiffly from the wiry hair that he had because he was a daddy. Ashley knelt and opened her mouth, and her daddy put his

cock inside it. Ashley did her best to bob her head to make her daddy's penis feel good, and she thought she had started to get the hang of it because Wes said "Good girl" several times before he held her head still and moved his hips the same way he did when his penis was in her vagina.

Then he said, "Here it comes, honey. Get ready. You're going to swallow daddy's seed now." He held himself in deep and she felt his hard penis pulse, and the stuff came out. It was a little bitter and very thick, but when she had been a good girl and swallowed it all, Wes said, "Thank you, honey" as he pulled his penis out.

"You're welcome, daddy," Ashley whispered.

"Go on into the bedroom now and do what I told you, please. It'll be a little while before I'm ready to fuck you, now that I've come in your mouth, but you were such a good girl that I'm going to give you your reward before that, instead of after."

Ashley felt her face go red at this news. He had said that thing about *kissing* her down there, which seemed like it might be the most embarrassing thing in the world. More embarrassing than kneeling in the kitchen to suck his penis; more embarrassing even than having a piece of ginger in her bottom. Of course it also seemed like the thing that might feel better than anything else in the world, too—but that almost made it more embarrassing, at the thought of how she would squirm and writhe with the pleasure her daddy made her feel.

Wes made her wait, thinking about it over the pillows, for at least five minutes, with the ache building and building between her spread legs, where she could feel the air shamefully moving—not letting her forget that she wore nothing but an apron and that her pussy had been shaved, and that her daddy had made her lie down like this to wait for him to kiss her in the naughtiest way possible.

Then she heard his step, and he said from very close behind her, "I'm so glad I shaved you, honey. It's such a pretty pussy, and now I can see how sweet and naughty you

are down there." She felt his weight descend on the bed, between her legs. The thought that he now looked at her most private places at such close range, while she herself must look at the blue comforter, seemed even more wicked than it had felt that morning to hold herself open while he shaved her.

"Your pussy looks very wet, young lady."

"Yes, daddy." She felt a tiny thrill at having to admit to the naughty way he made her feel.

Then she felt what could only be the tip of his tongue, flicking gently against her clit, and the pleasure shot through her body so forcefully that she let out a cry of pure pleasure that sounded like one of agony. Her daddy's tongue flicked and licked, and the lightning of ecstasy did make her writhe over the pillows, lewdly presenting herself for more of his attention. She cried out over and over.

Wes stopped for a moment, and she heard him chuckle. "Hold still, honey," he said with mock severity. "Daddy can hardly kiss you where he wants, you're squirming so much."

"I'll try, daddy," Ashley said, the heat coming again into her face. She did try, and the struggle to hold still seemed to add to the strength of the pleasure in her sinews. She came, and then she came again, hardly knowing whether she wanted any more of it but loving Wes for not giving her a choice in the matter.

Then he stopped, though, and said. "You got your daddy hard again, honey, with all that wriggling and those cute noises. Daddy's sorry, but he's going to fuck you for a long time now, because he already came in your mouth in the kitchen."

And then he did, without speaking further: he got on the bed and fucked her pussy from behind, while she wore her apron and she said, "Oh, daddy" and "Please, daddy."

Then he put the slippery stuff on and in her bottom, and she had to push so that her daddy could have anal sex with her. She felt so full of cock that it took her breath away, but her anus also still itched and burned from the ginger.

Somehow it felt so very right to be fucked there, after her figging, that though she could tell she would be very sore because of how hard Wes thrust, surging in and out with abandon in search of his release, it still somehow felt good.

"Such a nice bottom to pound, honey," he murmured as he came closer and closer, his own voice thick now with his exertions inside her. "So nice to have you like this."

And then her daddy came in Ashley's bottom with a shout, pushing in all the way until she thought she might faint with all the sensation. He held himself there for a long moment, and then he said, "Thank you, honey. That felt so good."

"Thank you, daddy," Ashley replied, suddenly having the urge to say something wicked. "I want to be your good little girl with my bottom and my pussy and my mouth, and make your cock feel good."

Wes laughed. "You're doing a very good job so far," he said, pulling slowly and gently out, and kissing her on each bottom-cheek, so that she giggled and blushed.

CHAPTER SIXTEEN

Late that night, while Ashley washed her panties in the sink—a task of which he was very happy to remind her so that he could watch her face get red yet again—Wes walked up the driveway to check on his phone whether he could find anything in the news about her escape.

None of the several stories he found about Tall Oaks concerned Ashley, though. Or, although Ashley's escape was mentioned, they didn't name her, and they didn't focus on her.

Rather, they concentrated on an investigation the state attorney general had opened into the process by which the correctional services corporation that currently ran Tall Oaks had obtained the contract, and possible abuses inside the facility. Wes wondered what part if any Ashley's parents had had in shifting the focus of law enforcement's interests so quickly. In the third story he read, he found a paragraph that read,

John Lewis, a Westchester County executive and the father of an eighteen-year-old girl who went missing from Tall Oaks on Friday, said that he hoped the investigation might uncover the reasons his daughter was allowed to escape. "All we want, though, is to have our

daughter back, and to make sure this doesn't happen to any other parent."

He also wondered what in the world he should do about it. He hoped Ashley's parents were really worried about her, but everything Wes had seen of her before he had taken her in hand seemed to indicate a family where status mattered a great deal more than affection. He had known people like that, growing up—even in the Midwest. They might not be *happy*, exactly, to send Ashley back to some other, better juvie, but if it meant they themselves came out clean as a whistle, they might very well not hesitate to sacrifice the years of their daughter's life that she should be using to figure out who she really wanted to be, and with whom, on the altar of respectability.

Wes couldn't take that risk.

"Did you find anything out, daddy?" Ashley asked as she snuggled into his arms, wearing again the big red t-shirt that Wes thought he would probably always remember her in, come what may.

"Mmm-hmm," Wes hummed into her sweet-smelling chestnut hair.

"What, daddy?"

"There's an investigation, honey. We need to figure out what you're going to do about it."

"Oh. What kind of investigation?" He heard the fear start to creep into her voice.

"About the facility and the company who was running it."

"Please don't make me…" Her voice trailed off into his bare chest.

"Don't make you what, honey?"

She sniffled. "I don't even know, daddy. I just… I just want to stay here with you, okay?"

Wes smiled and held her closer. Yes, he was definitely falling in love with her, if he wasn't already there. That would pose its own challenges, but right now it just felt

good to be able to say, "Okay, honey. I promise I won't let them take you away. We'll see what happens."

• • • • • • •

What happened, for the next two weeks, was nothing. The story vanished from the headlines, and on both his own instinct and Ashley's plea, Wes didn't try to make contact with her parents.

That decision felt like the easiest one he had ever made, because he and his little girl could hardly have been happier together if they were living in a four-star hotel or a palace. The rough little cabin Wes had built with his own hands became the scene of a domestic bliss so complete and so sealed off from the rest of the world that when Wes went to the big-box store an hour away, to buy groceries and some clothes for Ashley, the trappings of civilization seemed exotic and unreal.

When he presented Ashley with her new panties, white cotton of the kind worn by little girls everywhere, she giggled and blushed. Of course it meant the end of the nightly panty-washing he had enforced on her after she had ridden her daddy's cock like a rocking horse until he had spurted uncontrollably into her womb, or he had fucked her bottom until she begged her daddy to please come because she couldn't bear any more of his driving cock in her little anus, as well trained as that anus had already gotten from his use of it. But it also meant that when he took down his little Ashley's panties to play with her shaved pussy and her sweet, pert bottom, or to punish her, the underwear itself that he removed made his cock hard as an iron bar.

Ashley wasn't spanked daily, but she did have to go over her daddy's knee more than Wes thought she might have done if a big part of her didn't yearn for the boundaries he set with his firm hand on her little cheeks. She never failed to do the dishes, now, but she would forget to put them away, or she would forget to get the laundry started. Or,

even though Wes told her exactly when he wanted lunch every day, she wouldn't have started it when he got in from the workshop, and would be playing a game or doing a crossword instead.

Sometimes she would sass him, too, when he asked her to do something. "In a minute!" she said several times, until he cured her of it. When she said "In a minute!" Wes simply got the straight-backed wooden chair from the kitchen and put it in the living room, while Ashley stood watching with a furrow on her brow.

"I'm sorry, daddy," she would say. "Please, no spanking?"

"Come here, young lady. I've told you before that that tone is unacceptable, and your panties have to come down so that daddy can make it clear to you that good girls don't talk to their daddies that way. This time, I'm going to make sure you can't sit down for a day or two. You need to learn your lesson."

"Please, no, daddy. I promise."

"Are you going to come get over my knee, or do I need to put you there?"

That time—the last time for *in a minute!*—he did need to get her, because she tried to run to the door. Wes was quicker, though, and he marched her back to the living room, sat in the chair, and pulled her over his knee, where he summarily took down her jeans and her new white panties and began to spank her so hard that she sobbed from the very beginning.

"Please, daddy. Please, daddy," she wailed, but Wes held her between his thighs, with his left arm over her back, and spanked her harder than he ever had before, until her whole backside was red as a tomato.

That was the end of the sass for several days, and Ashley indeed couldn't sit for a full twenty-four hours. When the time came for sex that night, and Wes thrust into her sopping wet pussy from behind, his hips slapping hard against her well-punished bottom, she cried out much more

in pleasure than in pain.

But then, just as they reached the two-week mark, the sass came back, for something as simple as passing the pepper grinder.

"Get it yourself," she said. "Your arm is longer than mine."

Wes looked into her eyes, and saw to his surprise that his little girl wasn't joking; she really did mean to be bratty—really did want to push the boundaries. She had been in her new panties for four days, now, and he had been noticing a subtle shift in her behavior—she called him *daddy* a little less frequently, he thought, and she seemed a little less passionate under his hands and cock in bed.

"Tomorrow," Wes said, "you're going to have a switching for that disrespect."

The color drained from Ashley's face in the light of the setting sun that streamed onto the little table by the window.

"What? Oh, daddy, no." All her lost respect and obedience seemed to rush back into her demeanor. "Please. Please, just a spanking. I'm sorry. I've... I don't know what's gotten into me, but... not a switching." Wes looked at her steadily, not speaking. "I'll... I'll... I mean, maybe you can do the thing with the ginger again? Or..." She went from white to bright red in an instant. "Or the big black plug?" she whispered.

Wes had shown her the punishment plug a few days before, when she had protested that she didn't want him to train her anus that night. At the sight of it Ashley had said that, yes, she would like the little pink plug very much.

"No, honey. I think I know what's going on. Now that it looks like we're going to be together like this for a good long while, your psyche is starting to seriously adjust, and you're unconsciously rebelling a little. You need me to send you a message loud and clear that this is your life now: you're a taken-in-hand little girl, whose daddy gives the discipline you need to be happy. You'll have the punishment plug, too, but not until you've had a switching to teach you

the meaning of real old-fashioned discipline. Tomorrow morning you'll go out and find a green branch for me to switch you with. Then you'll take off your clothes and lie over the chair, and I'll whip your bare bottom the traditional way."

Tears stood in her eyes and her nose twitched as they dropped down her cheeks. "I'm so scared, daddy."

"You should be," Wes said, knowing that he had to make this boundary one that would stand very tall in her memory. "A switching is a serious thing. It's going to hurt, and you're going to remember it. But daddy will comfort you tonight, and he'll comfort you after your punishment. You already know in your head that it's for your own good, honey. Afterward, you'll feel that in your heart, too."

While Ashley did the dishes, Wes walked up the driveway again to read his email and check the news. He had stopped expecting anything about Ashley or Tall Oaks, but to his surprise he found that the story had suddenly come back to life.

Attorney General Preparing to Drop Tall Oaks Investigation

According to several sources inside her office, Attorney General Heather Bradshaw is close to a final decision that there is not enough evidence against the company running the Tall Oaks Juvenile Correction Facility to pursue a prosecution. "We're certain that abuses have occurred," said one source who spoke on condition of anonymity, "but it's very frustrating. No one will come forward."

Wes walked back to the cabin slowly and thoughtfully. He found Ashley still sniffling as she dried the plates and silverware, but also with a contrite, submissive look on her face that convinced him he had done the right thing in promising her the switching. As soon as she heard him come into the kitchen she put down the dishcloth and came into his arms.

"I'm so sorry, daddy," she said. "I know I need your discipline."

Wes held her tightly. "I'm glad you can see that, honey." He could tell that she meant to make another request for mercy, and he prepared to steel himself against it.

"Couldn't I have the switching over my panties? Please?"

"No, honey," he replied with a sigh. "You know how important bare-bottom discipline is in my house." With a surge of affection, he realized how much he wanted to say *our house* instead of *my house*. Well, what he had to say now might mean that he could start saying it.

"Yes, daddy," his little girl sniffled into his chest.

"But, Ashley," he said, changing his tone so that she would know they were about to talk about an adult real-world thing, "I saw some news we have to talk about."

"News?" she asked sharply, the sniffles gone.

"Uh-huh," Wes said, holding her gently away from him so that they could look into each other's eyes. "I think the attorney general needs your help. They're about to drop the investigation into Tall Oaks because no one will come forward."

A look of concern appeared on her face, and then she seemed to understand fully what Wes meant. "But if I…" She sucked her lips between her teeth as her creased brow showed how quickly her brain had started to work. "If I come forward, I'll have to go back. And maybe they'll put me in an adult prison!"

"Yes," Wes admitted. "So here's what I think, and I don't think you should make up your mind about it until tomorrow."

As if at the memory that she was going to be punished tomorrow, Ashley flinched.

Wes continued, "I think I should call a lawyer, have him or her contact the attorney general, and try to make a deal."

"But won't they know, then? Won't they be able to find me?" He could hear panic in her voice, and she started to tremble.

"I don't think so. I think attorney-client privilege will take care of that. But, yes, I think there's a risk. But, honey,

you can't stay a fugitive forever. I want you to let me do this. If you don't, I think I should get you back to your parents so they can help you as best they might."

"But they'll catch me then, too!" Ashley said in a quavery voice.

"They might. But at this point, as much as I'd like to keep you here with me, it would be selfish, and I think we would both keep thinking about it. It wouldn't work. I promise that if you let me call a lawyer, I'll stick by you. I'll stick by my little girl forever. This will be our house, even if you have to leave it for a while."

"So that's the decision? Stay and let you call a lawyer… and, you know…" her nose wrinkled in distaste, "…get a switching?"

Wes nodded. "Or I take you back to your parents."

Ashley took a deep breath and nodded herself, though her brow remained clouded.

"I'll talk it through with you all night if you want," Wes said.

That made Ashley smile, but her next words caught him a little by surprise. "And if your little Ashley just wants her daddy to fuck her hard, and then hold her tight?"

"Well," Wes said slowly, grinning, "we can do that, too, honey."

CHAPTER SEVENTEEN

Wes made breakfast for her in the morning, and let her sleep in and then stay in bed, thinking about the decision she had to make.

She could go back to her parents. She *could*. What would they do if Ashley showed up on their doorstep? Ashley spent a few minutes trying to come up with an answer—some idea of what it would look like to them, to see their daughter standing there, trying to recover her Westchester pride, trying to look and to feel like she belonged in her old hometown, in front of the house she had called home all her life until the accident.

But she had no idea, really. Westchester seemed to her as distant as the moon. Her father would either try to send her to some other country, she supposed, or he, too, would call a lawyer—probably without requesting permission the way Wes had.

Her father—and her daddy.

Under the covers, Ashley curled up into a ball, trying to make going home look palatable to herself. She didn't want to have to talk to the attorney general, or to whomever, and probably have to testify in court. And above all she didn't want a switching, no matter how completely unable she had

been the night before—while Wes held her knees up and open and pounded his cock into her, looking down into her eyes—to stop imagining what it would be like when he laid her over the chair and whipped her with the tree branch he had made her choose and cut until, when Wes told her to play with her clit for him, she had come and come and come with the fantasy of the switching driving her from ecstatic peak to ecstatic peak until she felt she would never be able to breathe again.

Why had she bratted like that, about the stupid pepper grinder? This whole thing would be easier without the switching looming over her, wouldn't it?

Easier, maybe, but not as… not as… what? Something about the terrible anticipation of having to cut her own switch in the woods, and bring it to her daddy so that her daddy could whip her naked bottom with it felt not easy, but… right.

Her Navy SEAL daddy, who knew how to take a girl in hand, how to punish her for her own good, how to spank her over his knee so that she learned to be a better girl for him and a better person in the world. Wes Garner, who had saved the girl overseas and paid the penalty; little Ashley's daddy, with the pain behind his eyes that seemed to disappear when he held his little girl in his arms.

She had sassed him terribly, even though she knew that being a brat always had consequences in his house, the little cabin where despite being a fugitive from the law Ashley had known more happiness over the last two weeks than she had had in her entire life to this point. Shouldn't she have a switching, for the disrespect she had shown her daddy?

If she took her punishment like a good girl, and she did the right thing to help the girls at Tall Oaks, it would start something big. Wes would stand by her, and it would start their real relationship. Her parents and the rest of the world would know that she had shacked up with a Navy SEAL in the woods. They would, probably and hopefully, soon know

that her furniture-making Navy SEAL daddy had a put a baby in her tummy.

Ashley felt sure that Wes would ask her to marry him, but that didn't even feel all that important to her. What mattered was being his little girl, and learning to please him more and more every day in this old-fashioned world where naughtiness received its just reward in very short order and daddy told you when it was time to have sex, and how you would have sex that night.

Still curled up, still with the comforter over her head, she felt her cheeks get hot at that thought, even as a little smile crept onto her lips and she had to suppress a giggle.

Not the easy decision, but the right one. She thought suddenly of the warden at Tall Oaks, of how his horrible threat of the paddle didn't seem to inhabit the same universe as Wes' promise of the switch, and she knew exactly what she had to do.

• • • • • • •

"Be careful when you're opening it," Wes said, handing her his pocket knife. "Hold it like this, and open it like this." He showed her twice. "Now show me."

Ashley took the lovely, very masculine thing, with the handle that seemed made of bone, and tried. Daddy had made it look very easy to open, but she realized that must be because his hands were so strong. Still, she managed to open the three-inch blade safely.

"Good girl. Show me again."

Ashley did. At least the business of the knife took her mind off the task she must now perform with it in the woods. But that distraction didn't last much longer.

"Alright," her daddy said with satisfaction in his voice. "Go cut your switch. Green wood from a tree, two or three feet long. It needs to be as thick as your finger, at the end where you cut it. If I have to send you back for another one, you'll get ten more. When you're choosing, and when you're

stripping off the twigs and leaves, I want you to think about what you did, and what you need to do to be a good girl for your daddy in the future, now that we're going to be together for a good long time."

A good long time. Ashley managed a weak smile despite the way her body trembled at the thought of the punishment in store.

"Forever, daddy?" she asked softly.

"If that's what you want, honey," Wes said. He plucked the knife gently from her hand and put his arms around her, the same way he had done when she had come out of the bedroom an hour before, in the red t-shirt and white cotton panties and said, "Daddy, I'll take my switching."

He held her silently for a long moment, and then he said, "You know what I hope?"

"What, daddy?" Ashley asked, mystified.

"I hope I made a baby in your tummy last night."

Ashley giggled. "Really, daddy?"

"Really, honey. I think you're going to be a wonderful mommy."

She smiled, then thought of something. "Won't it be hard… with little kids around to… you know, to take me over your knee?"

Wes chuckled. "You'll have to come to the workshop for your spankings," he said.

Ashley wondered why the prospect of having to go to Wes' workshop to be punished seemed to make her heart feel light. She decided she would spend a good long time trying to figure it out over the next few years.

"Oh," she said, burying her nose in his flannel shirt. "Okay, daddy."

"Time to cut your switch, honey," Wes said gently, holding her away from him again and putting the knife back in her right hand. "I'll see you in a few minutes."

Ashley took more than a few minutes, though, wandering through the woods. She felt sure that Wes wouldn't mind if she spent some extra time thinking about

what she'd done, and what she would do. She had sassed him at the dinner table, she finally decided, because she had started to feel things becoming serious between them, and she hadn't been able to see how being his little Ashley could go along with a serious relationship.

By earning herself a switching—the punishment that made her whole body shake as she thought about it, that would mean she couldn't sit down for days, that would leave welts for her to look at thoughtfully in the mirror as she remembered the stern lesson daddy had needed to give her—she had answered her question. Wes meant to be Ashley's daddy even after he had made her a mommy. He would spank her, switch her, and do just what he wanted to her with his cock, not just for a few weeks or months, but for the whole future: their future they would share.

She paused as she wandered, coming into a little glade and stopping there to look up at the blue sky overhead. She saw a sapling just in front of her, and her heart beat faster as she saw that it had branches about the thickness of her fingers. *Oh, no.* She had been out in the woods for twenty minutes, now, but until she saw the sapling she hadn't really been paying attention to the trees at all.

She had said the silly thing about the pepper grinder. She had disrespected her daddy, the man who had asked her above all to respect him. She had done it for no apparent reason. Little Ashley had earned a switching on her bare bottom.

Mechanically, she opened the knife. She took hold of the slim trunk with her left hand while with her right, being very careful to cut downward, she began to take not the slimmest of the branches—because Ashley really, really didn't want to be sent back out for a thicker switch—but maybe the next thinnest.

It only took a moment, and the branch, three feet long with four or five leaved twigs sticking out, was in her hand. She tried to think about how to be a good girl while she stripped away the twigs, exposing the springy green wood

underneath, but all she could think of really, was how this branch would feel when her daddy brought it down on her naked rear end.

"There you are, honey," Wes said with a little severity in his voice when he opened the workshop door at her knock. "I thought you might be dawdling."

"No, daddy," Ashley said, feeling her nose twitch with rising tears. "I was thinking, the way you told me."

Wes smiled. "Alright," he said. "I hope you came up with some ideas about how to be a good girl."

"Yes, daddy."

Wes' eyes went to the branch in Ashley's hand, which she held out to him. "That looks just fine," he said, taking it and the knife. He looked the switch over with a critical eye, then opened the knife and, while Ashley watched, whittled the end a little to make it smooth and very springy. Ashley watched with wide eyes, breathing more and more quickly as she saw her daddy getting the switch ready so that he could punish her with it.

Wes put his knife in his pocket, then he whipped the switch through the air twice. The sound made Ashley flinch each time, but it wasn't nearly as frightening as when her daddy turned and said, "Alright, honey. Into the house. All your clothes off, then lay yourself down over the chair in the living room with your bottom nice and high. Daddy's going to teach you your lesson now."

Ashley turned, the tears already starting to fall onto her cheeks, and walked to the cabin. She heard Wes' footfalls behind her, and she almost turned around to plead with him one more time to spank her, or to switch her atop her jeans or her panties, but she knew it would be absolutely in vain, and might get her extra cuts of the switch. When Wes decided to punish her, she had discovered, he made absolutely sure to carry through on the discipline he promised. The time she had learned not to say *in a minute* Ashley had thought he might just give her a token spanking, but his hand had visited her little cheeks with such force that

he really had, in the old phrase, quickly made her very sorry she had sassed him.

She opened the door, entered the cabin. She walked slowly to the bedroom, and heard Wes go to the living room and start to move the chair. Over the chair with her bottom nice and high. She blushed and trembled.

Somehow, though her hands shook, Ashley managed to pull off her t-shirt and unhook her bra. Somehow she even managed to take down her jeans and panties. Not consciously buying time, but unable to hurry toward the terrible moment of laying herself down for her whipping, she folded her clothes.

"Ashley, get your backside in here," she heard Wes call. "No dawdling. We need to get this over with."

"Okay, daddy," she called back, dropping the clothes on the bed and seeing how violently her hands trembled. Could she really go into the living room, naked, and take her switching like a good girl?

But her feet carried her. She had to get this over with, like her daddy said.

He stood next to the chair, on which he had put one of the couch cushions. *To raise my bottom.* Also, though, Ashley supposed, to make her more comfortable.

And though he held the switch in his right hand, he had something else in his left. As if seeing her notice what he had, he said, "You may hold this while I whip you, honey, and while I put the black plug in your bottom afterward. I got him when I bought you your new clothes, but I didn't find the right time to give him to you until now."

It was a teddy bear. Ashley felt her face crumple as she quickened her step and took the dark brown furry, sweet thing, and looked into its kind eyes. She clutched it to her chest and looked up at Wes.

"Thank you, daddy," she whispered.

"Over the cushion now," he said. "It's time to learn your lesson."

Ashley bit her lip, turned, and bent over the chair. With

his hand on her naked back and then on her bare bottom, Wes positioned her for punishment, making sure her the little globes rose higher than the rest of her.

"I'm going to switch you soundly, now, Ashley," he said, "and then I'm going to put the punishment plug in your bottom. I need to make sure you understand how important it is to respect your daddy."

Ashley heard the switch, and the sound frightened her so much that she cried out even before she felt the burning line across the center of her backside. But the sound immediately came again, and another burning line, and then she was screaming and thank goodness the fear had gone because she knew now just how awful a switching felt, and while it was a lot more painful even than one of Wes' spankings it wouldn't kill her, and neither would the big black plug.

Ashley's daddy switched her bottom the same way he spanked it: hard and fast and clearly intending that his little girl would feel thoroughly punished. The switching seemed to go on and on, while Ashley screamed and cried for it to be over, but teddy, held against her face with her left hand while she held onto the chair with her right, did make it better, wet as his fur became with her tears. She kicked at first, but it seemed her daddy felt no compunction about switching her legs, too, when she did that, which was even more painful than the thin branch felt on her bottom.

She heaved great sobs into teddy's fur, but she finally lay still for the switch, until her whole rear end, both her bottom and her upper thighs, felt like she had been stung by a nest of hornets. Then at last it had stopped, and her daddy was lubing her anus to prepare her for the punishment plug. That hurt, too, and it made her punished bottom feel so full that she wailed as her daddy put it inside her, but she still had teddy, and she kissed him, and she wondered whether her daddy intended to make use of the incredible ache he seemed to have created between her legs in the aftermath of the switching.

There must be a wet spot on the cushion, now, she thought. And surely he could tell that the way she cried out into teddy's fur had become very ambiguous. Ashley couldn't say that she really enjoyed anal sex, but she loved the way it made her feel so submissive to her daddy's pleasure, and the way he seemed to love to do it to her. Where had he gone? Was he still standing behind her? Didn't he want to put his hard penis in her bottom now? Wouldn't that be the best way to finish her lesson, and to teach her to respect him? She never felt as thoroughly mastered as she did when he rode her bottom to his cock's content.

She shifted on the cushion a bit, to try to soothe the pain of her bottom-cheeks, and she couldn't help moaning at that pain and the fullness of her bottom with the plug. She kissed teddy, wishing she could kiss her daddy. Wishing she could kiss her daddy's cock, to show she had learned her lesson.

How could she feel so unbelievably sexy after that terrible punishment? Was it all part of the mystery of how Wes had changed her so thoroughly in so little time? Just two weeks to an utterly new Ashley? She squirmed, and moaned again.

"Young lady," came Wes' voice from behind her, "you're making some rather wicked sounds."

Ashley felt her mouth twitch into a smile, and though she knew Wes couldn't see her face she tried to suppress it so that she could play her part better. "I'm sorry, daddy."

"How can you be so immodest after a switching, and when the punishment plug is still in your bottom?"

"I don't know, daddy." Then she cried out, because her daddy had put his hand on her bottom, over the base of the plug and on the burning cheeks he had whipped so severely.

"What should we do about the naughty state you're in, honey? You took your switching very well. I don't think I can let you come, but would you like to have daddy's cock in your bottom instead of the plug?"

Now Ashley couldn't suppress the smile. "Yes, daddy."

"Alright, honey," her daddy said. "Hold your teddy tight, because daddy is very hard, and he's going to come very deep inside his little girl's bottom."

He helped her push out the plug, and then he dropped his jeans and entered her immediately. She cried out into her new bear's fur as he took firm hold of her hips and rode her hard and deep. It felt like punishment and reward in one, and when Wes shouted and she felt his seed pulse inside her, Ashley knew she had indeed learned her lesson, as strange as the lesson might have seemed to the girl who had run through the woods to come crashing down in front of a speeding truck.

EPILOGUE

Ashley's parents wouldn't have anything to do with her, of course, when they found that their daughter was happily married and happily pregnant in a cabin in the woods. That probably made it easier for the lawyer to negotiate the probation deal with the attorney general, since upstate resentment against Westchester County aided the affair, and word of the noble circumstances of Wes' court-martial filtered out to the media.

She did have to attend a lot of depositions in Albany, to which Wes drove her and through which he sat patiently as she answered question after question. The whole experience was so stressful that cuddling and very straightforward sex—made even more straightforward by Ashley's sweetly growing tummy—made the fabric of their lives together. Wes spanked her when she sassed him, because he knew she did it to get the spanking, but he didn't do it very hard at all because of the baby.

Because she was pregnant, too, he did all the chores with his military efficiency, which gave Ashley no chance at all to misbehave, much as the tension cried out for some release in punishment.

After they found out, though, that Ashley wouldn't

actually have to testify at a trial, because the corporation that had run Tall Oaks had pled out and paid a huge fine, the messy mixture of emotions got the better of her.

"Goddammit, Wes," she said at the dinner table, "get the pepper grinder yourself."

Wes hadn't asked for the pepper. He looked at her with widened eyes and furrowed brow, as if wondering if the pregnancy, now in its eighth month, had driven her crazy at last. Then he seemed to remember about the pepper.

"Does someone need a spanking?" he asked. "Does little Ashley need to have her panties taken down over her daddy's knee?"

Ashley felt her mouth twist to the side. "I wish, daddy," she said, and then to her surprise she started to cry. "Promise me you'll put me over your knee and spank me hard after the baby comes?"

Wes grinned and got up from the table to take Ashley's hand and lead her to bedroom. "I promise, honey."

Ashley sniffled as she went. "Will you make me suck your cock, now, daddy?"

That made Wes snort. "Yes, honey. I think I'll do that. And then I'll make you come, much more than you want to."

"Good," Ashley said. "Little girls need to remember their daddies are in charge, don't they?"

THE END

STORMY NIGHT PUBLICATIONS WOULD LIKE TO THANK YOU FOR YOUR INTEREST IN OUR BOOKS.

If you liked this book (or even if you didn't), we would really appreciate you leaving a review on the site where you purchased it. Reviews provide useful feedback for us and for our authors, and this feedback (both positive comments and constructive criticism) allows us to work even harder to make sure we provide the content our customers want to read.

If you would like to check out more books from Stormy Night Publications, if you want to learn more about our company, or if you would like to join our mailing list, please visit our website at:

www.stormynightpublications.com

Made in the USA
Monee, IL
25 April 2025